ISBN 0-86163-310-5

Copyright © 1988 Award Publications Limited

First published 1988

Published by Award Publications Limited,
Spring House, Spring Place, Kentish Town,
London, NW5 3BH

Printed in Czechoslovakia

MANY MORE BEDTIME STORIES

by **Hayden McAllister**
Kay Brown
Jane Carruth

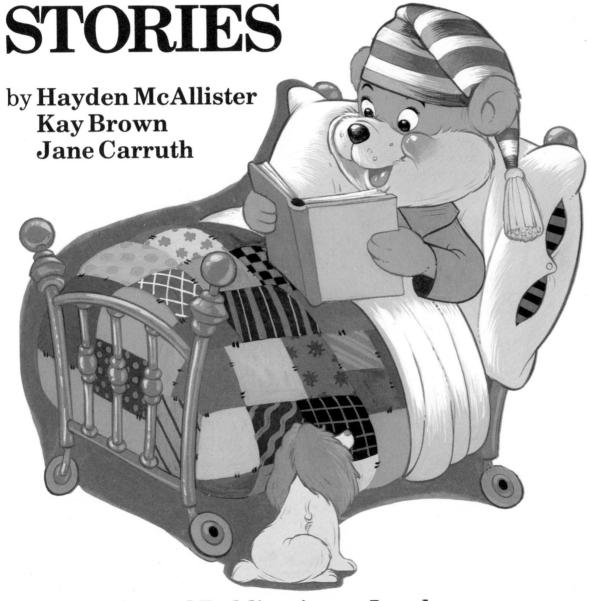

Award Publications – London

Contents

Bongo Bear

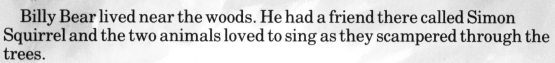

Billy Bear lived near the woods. He had a friend there called Simon Squirrel and the two animals loved to sing as they scampered through the trees.

One day Billy took two barrels of honey with him to the woods. Simon Squirrel quickly appeared from his treetop house to see his friend. The two sang their favourite songs for a while, but Billy soon became hungry and ate all the honey from the barrels, while Simon nibbled some acorns.

"I have an idea," said Billy. "Wouldn't our singing sound better if we had some music?"

"Yes," agreed Simon, "but we haven't any instruments!"

Billy turned the empty barrels upside-down between his knees and began to drum a tune on them. "These are my bongos," he explained.

Now, when Billy and Simon sing together, they beat out the rhythm on the bongo drums. What a clever bear!

Windy Hill Laundry

Rhoda the Rabbit lived in Big Tree Cottage on top of Windy Hill. Many of the rabbits who lived in the valley of Greengrass (at the bottom of Windy Hill), brought their laundry to Rhoda the Rabbit.

Rhoda the Rabbit liked doing the washing. She liked to see clothes looking really bright and clean. And when Rhoda had finished doing the washing, she would hang it up on the line on top of Windy Hill. Then the wind would come along and blow the laundry dry for her, giving the clothes a nice fresh smell.

When Aunty Rita Rabbit woke up and looked out of her bedroom window she was pleased to see the sun shining. Aunty Rita lived in a small white cottage near the river and, although she liked to look at the river, she was a little frightened of water.

But today her nephew Roger Rabbit was coming to see her. And he'd promised to take her out on the river in a boat. Just fancy! Actually floating on the water like a duck!

When Roger Rabbit arrived he was wearing his smart new hat. "I don't often wear hats," he said, "but it will keep the sun off my head."

"Then I'll take my sun brolly," said Aunty Rita. "Just in case it gets too hot."

In the afternoon after dinner, Roger took his Aunty Rita out boating. It was like a dream come true for Aunty Rita as she watched the river-bank drift by. They passed flowers and ducks and fish and Aunty Rita had a lovely time!

On the River

The Jungle Book

It was holiday time at the zoo and the animals were deciding what to do.

"Let's do something *together*," suggested Giraffe.

"Yes!" agreed Tiger. "We could hire a bus and go to the seaside."

"What a good idea, Tiger!" said Giraffe. "I've never seen the sea before."

Monkey nodded his head. "I'd like to come too," he said. "In fact, I could drive the bus."

So on the first day of their holidays, the zoo animals climbed on board their holiday bus. Monkey sat in the driver's seat, until the real bus driver arrived!

When they reached the seaside it was raining. But that didn't worry the animals. They decided to go to the cinema instead. When they arrived at the cinema they had a lovely surprise because *The Jungle Book* was showing.

"It's my favourite film!" cried Tiger.

"It's my favourite film too!" chorused Monkey and Giraffe.

Bubbles

Benny Bear had a bubble pipe. He liked to sit in his deck-chair and blow bubbles into the sky.

One day a little mouse called Millie came to watch Benny blowing bubbles. Millie enjoyed watching the bubbles floating into the air. So Benny gave her a tiny bubble pipe as a present.

Later, Millie brought her own little deck-chair and placed it beside Benny's big deck-chair. Then they *both* blew bubbles in the sunshine.

Charlie and Nipper

Charlie the Cat had been trying to catch Nipper the Mouse for years. Charlie was a *real* cat, and the one thing he didn't like was a clever little mouse like Nipper.

While Charlie was waiting outside Nipper's hole, Nipper the Mouse was painting a picture – of *himself*! When he'd finished it looked just like him!

"Now there are two Nippers!" he chuckled. "I'll stick this picture just inside my mouse hole," he squeaked to himself, "and while Charlie is keeping an eye on my picture – I'll nip out the back door and go and buy a cheese yoghurt."

When Nipper came back later, Charlie was still there, watching the picture.

"He'd make a good watch-dog!" chuckled Nipper.

15

The Dragon

Sir Roger lived in a castle near the Snowy Mountains. It was very lonely there and also very cold.

One day Sir Roger heard that a fierce fire-breathing dragon had moved into a cave in the Snowy Mountains. So Sir Roger put on his helmet, picked up his sword and went out to fight the dragon.

The fire-breathing dragon, whose name was Dumpty, was eating some grass when Sir Roger found him. When Dumpty the dragon saw Sir Roger with his sword he burst into tears. "Why does everyone hate dragons?" he cried. "I'm a peaceful, friendly dragon. And I've never hurt anyone in my life."

When Sir Roger heard this, he invited the dragon back to his castle. And as Dumpty was a fire-breathing dragon, Sir Roger gave him the job of lighting all the fires in the castle!

Farmer Joe

It was early morning in the farmyard. The sun had just risen and the rooster was calling.

Soon all the animals began to stir and make their way to the centre of the farmyard.

Billy the Bull ambled in and gazed over the wall. Shep the Sheepdog came into the yard. Farmyard Duck was there with her ducklings. Harry the Horse neighed good morning to his neighbours.

The sheep came in from the fields with their little lambs, and even Colin the Crow landed on the haystack nearby.

They were waiting for something, and listening too. But why. . . ?

Suddenly the farmhouse door banged and Farmer Joe came into the farmyard. He was whistling merrily.

"Quack!" cried the duck. "Baa baa!" cried the sheep. "Neigh!" neighed the horse.

"What a noise!" laughed Farmer Joe. "And all because you want your breakfast!"

17

Shep's Birthday Present

Some of the farmyard animals were attending a secret meeting. It was organised by Peregrine the Pig. (He liked organising things.)

"Right," whispered Peregrine the Pig. "Are we all here?"

"What's going on?" cried Harry the Horse. "Why is everybody whispering?"

"Not so loud!" said Red Rooster.

"Sorry," whispered Harry the Horse. "But why *is* everybody whispering?"

"We're wondering what to get Shep the Sheepdog for his birthday," said Hilda the Hen.

"I could lay him an egg," said Farmyard Duck.

"I don't think dogs like eggs," said Peregrine the Pig.

"Don't ask me," said Bernard the Bull, munching some hay. "I can't really think when I'm eating."

"I know!" said Harry the Horse. "Let's put some hay in his kennel. It'll make a nice mattress for him to sleep on."

Benny's Pigeon

Benny Bear had a pet pigeon called Feathers. Feathers lived in a pigeon house which Benny had built for him.

Feathers was very tame and he liked Benny to tickle the top of his head with an ostrich feather.

Three times a week, Benny Bear carried Feathers out into the country in a special basket. When they were a long way from home Benny opened the basket and let Feathers fly free. Feathers always soared up into the sky, circled once or twice and raced back towards home.

Before Feathers was out of sight, Benny would be running to the nearest bus stop to catch a bus home too.

If Benny arrived first he would put some peanuts in a bowl for his pet pigeon. Benny knew that it wouldn't be long before Feathers would come gliding out of the sky to eat his favourite meal.

19

Tennis Bears

Ben and Brian Bear had been sent tennis rackets and balls by their Uncle Bertie last Christmas, but so far they hadn't been able to play a single game!

The problem was that, although there was an ideal tennis court in the clearing in the wood, the bears didn't have a net to put across the middle. They often pretended to play, but it wasn't the same as a *real* game.

One night there was a terrible storm; the windows in the bears' house shook and the roof-tiles rattled. It was very frightening!

The next morning many of the woodland animals wandered into the sunshine to see what the wind had done. Ben and Brian walked to their special clearing, where they found the rabbits from their class at school looking very excited.

"Look, bears!" said one, jumping up and down. "Now you will be able to play tennis properly!"

Sure enough, right across the middle of the grassy clearing was a tree-trunk which the storm had blown down during the night. Now Ben and Brian can play *proper* tennis whenever they like.

The Little Bird

It was early spring when the little bird first visited Bob's garden. He would stand very still and feed her breadcrumbs and seeds from his hand – and soon the little bird grew quite tame. She liked to perch on the windowsill and sing a duet with Bob's pet budgie.

One sunny morning Bob was very surprised to see the little bird building a nest in a small bush at the bottom of the garden. For the next few days Bob and his budgie missed the cheerful little bird because she was so busy. Then Bob had a good idea. He very carefully moved the bush – with the little bird and her new nest – close to the window.

Now the little bird is sitting on five eggs in her cosy nest – but she still sings with Bob's budgie every day.

Old Bob Rabbit

Old Bob Rabbit was a watchmaker. He had a little shop in Bobtail village where he could mend clocks and watches.

Bob could fix big clocks, small clocks, wrist-watches and pocket-watches. He had once mended the famous church clock in Bobtail village after it had broken down.

Old Bob loved his work so much that he was not a good timekeeper. His wife, Mrs Mary Rabbit, became very cross because he was always late for dinner. So she made him set an alarm clock to tell him when it was time to close the shop and go home.

Musical Mouse

Musical Mouse had always wanted to conduct an orchestra. But so far no one had let him. They said he was much too small to be in charge of a *big* orchestra.

"Never mind," thought Musical Mouse. "I'll form my own little orchestra, and then we'll play some *great* tunes. We'll need a drum to go *bang bang*. And we'll need a trumpet to go *tah-rah tah-rah*. And a violin to go like ... whatever a violin goes like. And I'll be conductor."

So Musical Mouse gave a drum to Lion, a violin to Tiger, and a trumpet to Bear.

"Right!" said Musical Mouse, donning his best top hat and picking up his baton. "Now it's time for us to make music!"

"Great!" said Lion, dancing around and banging on his drum.

"Great!" growled Bear, dancing and blowing his trumpet.

Boris and Brian

Boris and Brian were two bears who were very good at thinking up new games to play with each other. One summer there was no rain for weeks and weeks. The river dried up completely and the riverbed became smooth and dusty. This gave Boris an idea for a new game.

He gathered some branches and carved skittles from the wood, and painted them different colours, and he asked Brian to find six smooth, round stones. Soon two bears were ready to play skittles.

They stood the brightly-painted skittles at one side of the dry riverbed. From the other side they bowled the shiny stones at the skittles, trying to knock them down. The new game was such fun that soon the other animals who lived nearby came to watch.

When the rain came again, Boris and Brian put their skittles and stones in a safe place – ready for the next dry summer.

Billabong the Kangaroo

One morning Billabong the Kangaroo was happily hopping through the trees on his way to school, singing, "One and one make two – I'm a kangaroo!"

The noise of his thumping feet woke up a sleepy butterfly, who called, "Hello! Where are you off to in such a bouncing hurry?"

"I'm going to school," said Billabong, proudly.

"Well, it looks as if you've forgotten your school books!" said the butterfly as he settled down again.

"Oh no," said Billabong, "I always carry those in my kangaroo pouch! One and one make two – I'm a kangaroo!"

Blackberries

Fenella and Fred were fieldmice who lived in a nest of grass and leaves under the roots of a great big cypress tree.

One autumn day when Fenella and Fred were scampering through the grass on their way back home, they stopped under a blackberry bush to rest.

As they were resting, a ripe blackberry fell beside them. Fred decided to taste the blackberry.

"It'll make a change from nuts and grain," he said. So he had a mouthful and found it was delicious. Fenella tasted some and she liked the taste too!

"We'll have to take two or three of the berries home with us, Fenella," said Fred. "Then you can make us both a tasty blackberry pie."

24

Bob's One-Man Band

Joe and Isabel were walking with their mum when they heard a sound like a brass band. Looking down the road Joe and Isabel were amazed to see that only one man was making the sound.

"It's Bob Busker and his one-man band," said Mum. "Go and give him this coin and ask him to play a tune for you."

Joe and Isabel ran down to where Bob was standing with his dog.

"And a jolly good day to you!" said Bob, rattling his tambourine.

"Please play us a tune, Mr Busker," said Isabel.

"Which tune would you like?" said Bob.

"Would you play 'How much is that doggy in the window'?" asked Joe.

"Well, that's my jolly little dog's favourite tune!" beamed Bob Busker. "Just you watch him wag his tail when I play it!"

Kitty the Kitten

Kitty the Kitten was always getting into mischief!

One afternoon Mum put Kitty out into the garden to play. First she chased Jim's clockwork mouse up and down the lawn. Then she chased the birds! When the birds flew up into a tree Kitty decided to climb up after them.

Of course the birds flew away, but when Kitty tried to climb back down the tree she found that she could not. She grew frightened and began to cry.

As soon as Jim and Julie heard Kitty miaowing they went out into the garden to see what was wrong. They saw that Kitty was stuck halfway up the tree.

Mum put a small ladder up against the tree trunk so that Jim could climb up and rescue Kitty. But once Kitty was back indoors she soon began getting into mischief all over again!

Benny the Dancing Bear

Benny the Bear's three favourite things were honey, singing and dancing.

Benny lived in a house at the foot of the hill. On top of the hill was a well.

Every morning after Benny had eaten his breakfast he would climb to the top of the hill with two buckets and fill them at the well.

The trouble was, Benny liked to sing and dance on the way down. So, when he arrived home, half the water had spilt out of his buckets!

When the local carpenter heard about Benny's problem, he made some wooden lids to fit on to the buckets.

Now Benny can sing and dance with his buckets, and he doesn't spill a drop of water. Well, perhaps just a little!

27

Night School

"It's about time some of us jungle animals learned to read," said Tortoise.

"There's not much time for reading," pointed out Lion, "because there's so much to do all day."

"And when we have got time to read," added Bird, "it's too *dark* to see."

"If only we had reading lamps like people have," cried the two Monkeys.

"I've got an old candle," boomed Rhino. "I found it under a gooseberry bush."

"Right!" said Lion. "If we can light the candle and stick it on the horn on your nose, Rhino, that should give us light to read our books by."

"Very well," agreed Rhino. "I'll act as our reading lamp *and* librarian."

"And we'll bring our book of bedtime stories," chorused the two Monkeys. "And we'll read you all a story about Aladdin and the magic lamp."

28

Star-Struck Mouse

Montague Mouse sleeps all through the day in his underground burrow of roots and leaves and straw. When night-time comes and darkness falls Montague Mouse eats some cheese, drinks a cup of rainwater and picks up his telescope.

Leaving his burrow, Montague scampers through the grass and climbs to the top of an old anthill.

On top of the hill is a comfortable toadstool. Here Montague sits for hours and gazes at the stars and the moon through his telescope.

Montague has seen many shooting stars whizz across the night sky. Once a shooting star passed just over Montague's head . . . and the next morning Montague's tail was glowing with starlight.

The Princess

A Princess had been born to the King and Queen of Happy Land.

The Princess was called Alice. Trumpeters played a fanfare from the castle walls. There was a firework display and flags were flown in honour of Princess Alice's birth. People sang and danced and rejoiced.

The animals in the castle grounds were happy too.

When Princess Alice slept in a yellow cot in the castle grounds, the animals came to see her.

"Isn't she pretty," said the young deer.

"She's a lovely baby. A real princess!" declared the rabbit.

"Let's gather a few flowers and decorate her yellow cot with them," suggested the squirrel.

A little bluebird helped lay the flowers on the hood of the cot. And a hedgehog arranged flowers at the base of the cot.

"A pretty cot for a pretty baby!" declared the rabbit.

Shipwrecked Fox

Ferdy the Fox was stranded on a tiny desert island. His boat had sunk and the only thing Ferdy had been able to save was his banjo and a big tin of boiled sweets.

But Ferdy didn't mind. It was nice to be away from the noise of the big city where he lived.

As he sat there under the single palm tree, playing his banjo, the sea made soothing noises as it lapped on the sand. Ferdy reached out and picked up a coconut that had fallen from the palm tree, and poured himself a drink of coconut milk.

"This is the life," said Ferdy, dipping into his tin of boiled sweets.

"Ugh!" spluttered Ferdy. "Peppermint! I *hate* peppermint! Why couldn't I be shipwrecked with a tin of chicken flavoured boiled sweets?"

Ice Cream Dream

Although Percy Podge liked marzipan, chocolate, nougat and sherbert – his favourite treat was ice-cream!

Percy had tried raspberry flavoured ice cream, vanilla flavoured ice cream, strawberry flavoured ice cream, chocolate flavoured ice cream, and he loved them all . . .

One night Percy Podge had an amazing ice cream dream. He dreamt he was eating the *biggest* ice cream you ever saw. The ice cream was actually bigger than Percy! In his dream, Percy ate every last mouthful of the giant ice cream.

When he woke up next morning Percy Podge was astonished to find that he was *still* hungry!

Sleepy Snail

Sarah Snail was crawling up a smooth, round stone near the river. "When I get to the top of this stone," Sarah thought, "I'll have a little sleep inside my shell."

Soon after Sarah had fallen asleep it began to rain. When she woke up Sarah found the river had come over the top of the bank and was all round her stone!

"Help!" cried Sarah. "I'm trapped!" Luckily, Dilly Duck heard the little snail.

"Don't worry, Sarah," quacked Dilly. "If you climb onto my back I'll take you safely to the bank."

After that Sarah was very careful not to fall asleep too near the river!

Baking Day

Mother Bear was baking. She had made some little honey cakes for tea, and now she was making bread. Laura Bear wanted to make a cake too. So her mum gave her a piece of dough. Laura rolled the piece of dough until it was flat. Then she moulded it into a teddy bear shape.

"I'll put it in the oven with the bread," said Mrs Bear. "When it has been baked it should turn golden brown."

"Oh good!" said Laura. "Then it will be just like a teddy bear!" When Father Bear came home, Laura gave the teddy bear to him.

"It's just what I've always wanted," said Father Bear with a smile.

Pilot Bear

Most people keep a car in their garage, but Basil Bear was different. He kept a red aeroplane in his garage.

Every summer's day, unless it was raining, Basil Bear would take his red aeroplane up amongst the clouds. He liked to look down on the houses and the treetops and the fields far below. If his friends saw him above they would wave to him as he passed overhead.

One particular friend, called Colin Crow, would fly up *above* the red aeroplane and then drop down and land on the tailplane. When Basil wanted to turn right, Colin Crow would put out his right wing. And when Basil wanted to turn left, Colin would put out his left wing.

When Basil wanted to go straight ahead, Colin Crow would just sit still and enjoy the feeling of being able to fly without the effort of having to flap his wings!

The Two Hippos

The two hippopotamuses lumbered down a country lane. It was a hot day. In fact it was a *very* hot day, especially for hippos who like the cool of the river mud. "Phew!" said one. "It's hot!"

"Phew! You're telling me!" said the other.

"Phew!" said one. "I'd like a nice cool plod in a nice cool river."

"Phew! You're telling me!" said the other.

"Phew!" said one, wiping his big forehead. "I'd like a nice crater full of ice-cubes and fresh oozy mud to slowly sink into. . . ."

"Phew! You're telling me!" said the other.

"Why do you keep saying 'Phew – you're telling me'?" asked one.

"Because it's phew! – too hot to argue," said the other.

"Phew! You're telling me!" said the first one.

Delia the Dove

Delia the Dove always liked flowers. A long time ago when she was a baby bird and couldn't fly, she fell out of her nest and landed on a soft bed of marigolds. Those marigolds saved her life.

Mr Jones liked marigolds too. He had a window-box at every window of his big white house, full of brightly coloured flowers.

Mr Jones also liked doves. One day Mr Jones met Delia the Dove as he was planting out some flowers in a window-box. She came and landed on the edge of the window-box with a sprig of heather in her beak. Mr Jones planted the heather in his garden, and it grew.

Every day after that Mr Jones would leave some peanuts in the corner of the window-box for Delia the Dove. Sometimes the children would wait at the other side of the window and watch her eat.

"Coo, coo, coo!" Delia would say, before flying away. "Thank you!"

Playing Marbles

Sam and Stewart were playing marbles in a quiet little corner of the park. There was a nice smooth piece of ground beneath the tree and Sam and Stewart felt it was the perfect place for a game of marbles.

At first it was only the two boys playing there in the shade of a huge tree. *Click, click,* went the marbles. "Good shot!" said Stewart.

A little kitten called Toodles thought it was an interesting game and came to watch.

Two little girls, wandering by, came over to see what the boys were doing.

"I don't know what this game is called," whispered one little girl.

"Marbles," said Sam. "They call it marbles. But girls don't often play."

A blue tit flew down to a lower branch of the tree to see what was going on. Then a squirrel joined the audience.

"I wonder if this game could be played with acorns?" thought the squirrel.

37

Acorn Soup

Sandra Squirrel had borrowed a **recipe** book from the Woodland Library. The first recipe in the book told her how to make acorn soup.

"I'll need one cup of water, six ears of wheat and some dried acorns," said Sandra. "I think I'll go to the wishing well to draw some water."

When Sandra arrived at the well she met Bertie Bird. "Oh! Hello, Sandra!" chirped Bertie. "I've just made a wish that someone will invite me to dinner."

"You're very welcome to come and try some of my acorn soup for your dinner," smiled Sandra.

Bob's Flowers

Bob the Bear had an empty honey barrel in his garden. First he painted it, and then he filled it with soil. In the springtime Bob bought some flower seeds and planted them in the soil. When summer came the seedlings grew. So Bob tended the seedlings and watered them when they were thirsty.

Now the old honey barrel is full of colourful flowers. Bob is really pleased, and so are Bob's friends, the honey bees, who come every day to visit the flowers.

Water Music

Tim Rabbit loved Lucy Rabbit, and Lucy Rabbit loved Tim.

Lucy lived in a lovely rabbit house in Yellow Sand Cliff. From her bedroom window she could see the sea.

One day Tim Rabbit came to visit Lucy. But before knocking on the door Tim decided to sing her a song. He was just about to start his song when Lucy emptied a bucket of water out of her bedroom window. Poor Tim got soaked! But Tim didn't mind. He still loved Lucy and Lucy still loved him.

"Next time I sing," he said, "I'll wear my raincoat!"

Windmill Bread

There was once a windmill and a baker's shop in the middle of Rabbitland. Three rabbits, Rodney, Rudolph and Rosie, lived in the windmill.

When the wind blew, the windmill sails moved and turned the millstones which ground the corn. With the corn, Rosie Rabbit made the bread and cakes which she sold in the baker's shop.

Rosie Rabbit baked such delicious bread that soon lots of rabbits came to the shop to buy it. In no time at all Rosie's bread became so famous that Rodney Rabbit bought a baker's van so he could deliver bread and cakes all over Rabbitland.

As for Rudolph Rabbit – well, he was just a baby rabbit who liked eating his mummy's cooking.

Sir Roderick

Roderick had been reading about knights in a book. He'd especially enjoyed the adventures of the Knights of the Round Table.

"We've got a square table at home," thought Roderick. "I'll call myself a Knight of the Square Table."

"What I need is a horse and a sword," decided Roderick. So he went into his playroom and sat on his rocking-horse.

"Oh dear! I've forgotten my sword!" he said. And he searched in the cupboard and found a wooden ruler.

"That's better," he smiled as he got back on his horse. "This ruler will do nicely as a sword."

Then Roderick frowned. "But from what I've read, knights always wear helmets, so I'd better wear one too." Roderick thought a moment. "I know! I'll borrow Mum's pan and wear that on my head as a helmet. And as we had baked beans for dinner she won't need it for a while."

And so Sir Roderick, Knight of the Square Table, wearing his helmet and sword, rode into battle...

Later Sir Roderick found an old broom which he used as a lance. The dustbin lid became his shield. Even before he had his tea, Sir Roderick had many more exciting adventures!

The Tidy Circus

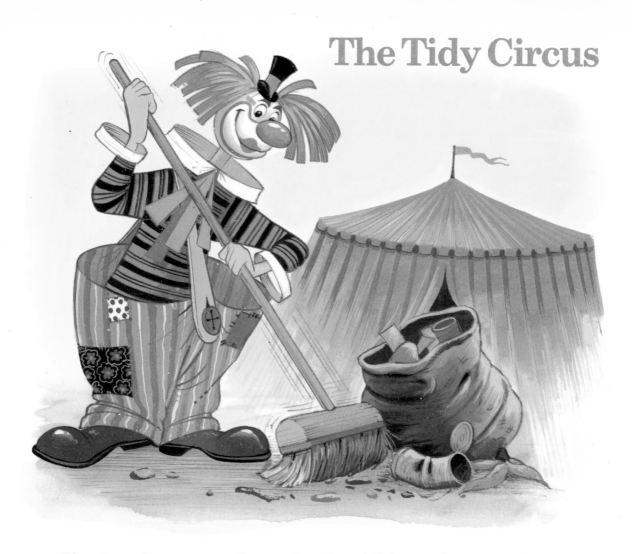

The circus fun was over for another day. All the performers and the animals had gone home to rest. The lights in the big tent had been turned off and all was silence. Only Poppo the Clown had stayed behind.

Poppo the Clown didn't know what to do with himself. So he went for a walk round the circus, whistling a tune as he strolled along. "Dumty-dumty-dee-dum."

The trouble was, Poppo kept tripping over drink cans which people had thrown away.

"I don't mind tripping over when people are watching me," he said. "Because that makes them smile. But I'd rather not trip over when I'm walking by myself. I know!" said Poppo. "I'll sweep up all the cans and the rubbish and put it all in a sack. Then I won't trip over when I'm strolling along!"

When Poppo had finished, the whole circus was so clean and sparkling that it seemed to be smiling. And Poppo was smiling too.

Tim and the Monster

The children at playschool had spent many weeks making a huge monster. It had a fierce face with spiky teeth, horns, rolling eyes, and a great big mouth! When it was finished the children named their monster Mr Dragon.

Mr Dragon was so long that eight children had to get inside the spotty skin to make it move! If you were inside the tail it was hard to know what was going on at Mr Dragon's front end, it was so far away!

Their teacher had been telling the children all about Saint George and the Dragon. Tim found a play-sword and asked if he could pretend to be Saint George and fight Mr Dragon.

When the children had hidden inside the monster's long body and Mr Dragon came wiggling towards him, Tim suddenly realised what a brave man Saint George must have been!

43

Captain Bodger's Friends

Captain Bodger had a boat which he called *The Seadog*.

He always kept *The Seadog* shipshape and ready to sail.

Sometimes Captain Bodger would get on his boat and go and visit his friends who lived out at sea.

There was a friendly whale called William who had once towed Captain Bodger back to harbour when *The Seadog* had broken down.

There were seagulls which liked to land on the cabin of *The Seadog* and talk to Captain Bodger about the weather.

Captain Bodger also knew a pelican called Pedro. Pedro the Pelican often perched on a post and sang sea songs in a pelican voice. When Captain Bodger heard Pedro sing, he would play along on his foghorn.

The Wet Mouse

Monty Mouse had been exploring the garden. He was searching for a cool, shady spot where he could escape from the heat of the sun.

The clump of big flowers in Lucy's garden was just what he was looking for! Monty curled up beneath the scented flowers and soon fell asleep.

Monty had only been asleep for five minutes when he felt drops of water falling on his furry head. When he stood up he realised that Lucy was watering the flowers.

"Hum! Now I'll have to go and sit in the hot sun to dry off!" muttered Monty.

Sammy the Seal

Sammy was a performing seal who worked in a circus. He could jump through a hoop and balance things on his nose.

One day at lunchtime, when Sammy was playing with his coloured ball, his trainer brought him a bucket full of fresh fish.

"Thanks," said Sammy Seal.

"You're welcome," said his trainer.

Sammy looked at the bucket of fish and thought a moment . . .

Next minute he was balancing the bucket of fish on his tail and spinning the ball on his nose.

Sammy Seal gently lowered the bucket and dropped the ball.

"How would you like to do that as your new circus act?" asked his trainer.

"Great!" said Sammy, clapping his flippers together.

High-Flying Kite

Sally had been given a new kite by her Uncle Fred. She was very excited and straight after dinner she went to the park to fly her kite.

It was a nice breezy day and kites of all shapes and colours were flying in the sky. But poor Sally couldn't get *her* kite to fly.

Her friend Johnny came along and he tried to help. But Sally's kite just wouldn't fly.

Suddenly Johnny had an idea! There was a man in the fields near the park who had a hot-air balloon. Johnny asked the man if Sally could go up in the balloon and fly her kite from the balloon basket.

The man agreed and Sally climbed into the balloon basket with her kite.

Once in the air, Sally's little kite flew perfectly. "It's obviously a high-flying kite," she said to herself.

Water-Skiing

Bob the Bear had been invited to visit his friend Ben for the weekend.

Ben the Bear lived by the seaside, so Bob took his water-skis along. On the first afternoon Ben hired a motor boat and both he and Bob went boating together.

The next afternoon, Bob put on his water-skis while Ben tied a length of rope to the back of the motor boat.

Ben started the motor boat and Bob hung on tightly to the rope. In no time at all Bob was whizzing along on his water-skis behind the motor boat.

"We'll have to do this more often," beamed Bob.

"Yes! Why not come down again next weekend," said Ben.

Home-Made Presents

Mary and her brother David liked to look in the window of the toy shop near their home. There was a cuddly teddy-bear which Mary thought was the best toy in the whole shop. David didn't agree; he liked the bright wooden truck better than anything else.

Mary and David wanted these toys for Christmas, but they knew their mother and father couldn't afford to buy them, so the children didn't say any more about them.

On Christmas morning, when breakfast was finished, the family gathered round the pretty tree in the sitting-room. Mary's parcel was round and soft – but David's was square and hard!

When Mary opened the paper she couldn't believe her eyes! There was a beautiful, cuddly teddy-bear – just like the one in the shop window. David's surprise was a red wooden truck, exactly like the one in the toy shop! Their clever parents had secretly made the toys after the children had gone to bed!

48

Bronco Bear

Bronco Bear wanted to be a cowboy. For his birthday his mum made him a cowboy hat.

Bronco's dad was a carpenter, and he made Bronco a wooden horse which had four wheels.

Bronco liked to take his horse into the garden and ride it up and down the lawn. He hoped that one day he would meet a *real* cowboy.

When dinnertime came, Bronco's mum made him some beans on toast, which was a *real* cowboy meal.

Jumping for Joy

Pickle dreamed of being a show-jumping champion. The trouble was, he was so tiny and his legs were so small, he really wasn't built to jump big fences. Pickle would gallop around his little field, jumping over daisies and tufts of grass, and pretend he was jumping over big fences.

One summer's day, a butterfly flew over the fence and into the field. "My goodness!" cried Pickle. "How I wish I could sail over that fence as easily as you. You see, I want to be a show-jumping champion."

"You look like a champion to me," said the butterfly. "So why not try and jump the fence now. I'm sure you can. I'll fly and whisper encouragement in your ear."

So Pickle ran and the butterfly flew towards the fence. Together they sailed over. "We'd make a good team," laughed Pickle, jumping for joy.

Raymond the Flying Rabbit

The crowd cheered as the circus master announced: "Ladies and gentlemen; we present Raymond the Flying Rabbit!"

Porky Pig rolled out the cannon with Raymond already packed inside. Everyone held their breath while Willie Mouse lit the fuse. There was a sizzle, a crackle and then a great big *BANG*!

The next moment Raymond the Flying Rabbit was flying through the air! (Inside his coloured waistcoat he wore his special rabbit parachute.)

One day Raymond hopes to be the first rabbit on the moon.

50

The Sad Frog

Mr Dragonfly saw a sad-looking frog sitting alone at the side of a pool.

"Cheer up, Mr Frog," said the dragonfly, as it hummed through the air.

"I can't," sighed Mr Frog. "I wish I could."

"What is wrong?" asked Mr Dragonfly, circling round the frog's head. "Perhaps I can help!"

"Wrong!" muttered Mr Frog. "The worst thing that could happen to a frog – that's what's wrong... I've lost my croak."

"Poor Mr Frog," soothed the dragonfly. "What do you think happened to your croak?"

"I think I must have forgotten *how* to croak," muttered Mr Frog.

"I'm sure you haven't," said Mr Dragonfly. "You just stopped croaking because you're not happy. I'll try and cheer you up."

With that the dragonfly landed on top of the frog's head and began to tickle him. Soon Mr Frog couldn't stop laughing. "Croak, croak," he said. "Croak, croak. Please stop tickling my head!"

Reading Lamp

Brock the Badger lived in a big, gloomy house underneath the ground.

It had always been too dark to read in Brock the Badger's house... until he met his friend Willie the Glow-worm.

Willie was a bright glow-worm in more ways than one. And he soon came up with a bright idea to help Brock the Badger read in the dark...

As Brock sat in his armchair with a book in his hand, Willie sat on top of the book and glowed brightly.

Hide and Seek

Porky Pig and his friends were playing hide and seek. They began their game after lunch and didn't stop until tea-time.

They all had such fun that, once tea was over and the washing-up done, they hurried outside to play hide and seek again!

Now Porky Pig was very good indeed at hiding, but not very clever at seeking. His friends seemed to find such mysterious places to hide in that, when it was Porky's turn to find them, it took a long, long time!

Soon it was quite dark; the moon and all the stars had come out but Porky still couldn't find anyone. He went into the house to fetch his torch.

"I know you're all hiding there somewhere!" Porky cried as he shone the torch into the bushes.

"Let's hope he finds us before the batteries in his torch run down," whispered one of Porky's friends to another. "Otherwise we'll be hiding here all night!"

Can you find the animals hiding in the picture?

The Six Rabbits

There were six rabbits who lived in a warren in the middle of a big meadow. They were all different sizes. One was tall, and he had a high voice. Another was small and round and he had a deep, low voice. All six rabbits could sing beautifully, and one day it occurred to them to form a choir.

Every Saturday afternoon the six rabbits would give a choir concert in the middle of the wood. Birds and mice and sometimes a hedgehog would come to hear them sing.

The six rabbits wrote their own words and music and they sang about trees and stars and birds and mice and hedgehogs...and rabbits!

53

Sidney Squirrel

Sidney Squirrel was having the time of his life! He was so full of energy he chose the tallest oak tree to climb. After scampering up the trunk he leapt from branch to branch – right to the top of the tree!

Then Sidney saw an acorn right at the end of the branch he was sitting on. It was the biggest acorn he'd ever seen in his life.

At that very moment the acorn dropped. Sidney Squirrel watched it go whizzing down to the ground. Then he scampered down after it.

"I've got a nice idea," beamed Sidney, picking up the acorn. "I'll go over and see Simon Squirrel in Tree Top Wood, and give this acorn to him."

Jogger Bob

Bob the Bear wanted to be a jogger.

Most bears walk. A few bears run; but Bob the Bear wanted to be *different*. So he bought himself some red jogging shoes and a jogger's headband.

He put on his tracksuit, laced up his jogging shoes and went out for a leisurely run.

Bob the Bear had jogged over a kilometre when it began to rain heavily. Poor Bob got soaked.

Before he reached home Bob was a waterlogged jogger.

54

The King's Pie

The King was very sad. "Nothing seems to cheer me up any more," he complained. "I have all the jewels and gold I want, but it doesn't make me happy."

The Queen called in the Court Jester, who told the King lots of jokes and tried to make him laugh. But the King didn't even smile.

"It's such a long time since I felt happy," sighed the King.

When Louise the kitchen maid heard that the King was sad, she baked him a nice steak and kidney pie.

Louise presented the hot steak and kidney pie to the King. When the King saw the delicious pie, he gave a great big smile.

"Thank you, Louise," he said. "That really has made me happy because it reminds me of the lovely pies my mother used to bake."

Funny Fishing

Snuffle the Dog and Ruby the Rabbit had gone out for a walk together.

"What a lovely day it is," said Ruby, as they strolled along. "Let's go down to the old stone bridge by the river and watch the sun dancing on the water."

"That sounds like a good idea, Ruby," agreed Snuffle. "I love sitting quietly on the river-bank."

When the two friends reached the old stone bridge they found Podgy the Pig there. Podgy was fishing from the bridge, and when Snuffle and Ruby looked over the side of the bridge they saw Podgy's sister Pandy swimming about in the water below. Both pigs were squealing and giggling and Snuffle asked them why.

"My tin whistle has fallen into the river," laughed Podgy, "and we're having great fun trying to fish it out again!"

Burt and the Drill

Burt Bear had found a pneumatic drill in his cellar. Just for fun, Burt thought he'd test the drill in his garden.

The noise from his drill was really awful! A squirrel in a nearby tree covered its ears with its paws to shut out the noise.

The drill bounced and shook and wobbled and, as Burt held on to it, it made his teeth rattle. Chunks of earth were flying everywhere. A moment later Burt's drill had burst an underground water-pipe and water spouted high into the air!

A little bird, perched on the fence, couldn't understand what Burt Bear was drilling for.

The truth was, that having switched on the great big drill ... poor Burt Bear didn't know how to switch it off again!

Loopy Lizard Wins Through!

One day Loopy Lizard met up with Harry Hare and the two, who did not like each other much, began to boast about how clever they were.

In the end Harry Hare said, "I challenge you to a race. And the winner is to be given a party."

"I accept," said Loopy, but he thought that he could never beat Harry in a straight race – no matter how hard he tried.

On the day of the race all their friends gathered at the winning-post. Loopy's friends couldn't help feeling sorry for him. He was such a jolly fellow, it seemed a shame that he was going to be beaten by stuck-up Harry Hare.

But it didn't turn out that way! At the very last moment Croaky Greenfrog, a master-hopper, offered Loopy a ride on his back. "There's nothing in the rules to say how you get to the winning-post," he chuckled. "I'll have you there in a couple of big hops!"

When Harry saw what Loopy was up to he was so furious that he said he wouldn't race at all. By the time his friends had persuaded him to change his mind, Loopy Lizard was nearing the winning-post. It only took a small hop for Croaky and Loopy to cross the line. Everybody cheered like mad – everybody, that is, except Harry, who refused to give a party!

"That's all right," cried Loopy, cheerfully. "The party is on me!"

Magic Carpet Music

Tom and Sally and Benji, their dog, were sitting on the fireside rug while their mother was making the dinner.

Tom was learning to play his trumpet. Sally was reading a story about a magic carpet, and Benji was yawning.

Suddenly Tom said, "Listen to this tune called 'Dream Time'." As Tom began to play his trumpet they all seemed to be floating away. Sally couldn't believe her eyes! She could see their house below and the green hills far away. She was wondering how they were going to get back home when Tom said, "Wake up, Sally. Dinner is ready."

59

Arthur's Boat

Arthur the Ant was skipping along through the wet grass one day when he found a walnut shell.

Arthur suddenly had a good idea. He tugged the walnut shell to the edge of a puddle. Then he searched around until he had found two matchsticks.

Arthur put the matchsticks into the walnut shell, pushed the shell into the puddle and climbed in.

Using the matchsticks for oars, Arthur rowed himself into the middle of the puddle.

"This is the life!" chirped Arthur." I will be able to come boating every day now!"

Musical Icicles

Samantha Squirrel lived in a hollow tree at the edge of the wood. Every morning she looked out of her window and thought how lucky she was to live in such a lovely place.

Early one winter day Samantha woke up and shivered. When she looked out she saw that the fields were covered with snow and there was a row of sparkling icicles hanging above her window. When she touched one of them with a spoon it made a pleasant ringing sound. Samantha soon discovered that, because they were different sizes, each one made a different note, so she played a tinkling tune on the icicles!

60

The Home Helps

Mopsy Bunny and her brother Michael wanted to earn some money so that they could buy their mother a proper birthday present. "We're not clever enough to get proper jobs," Michael said sadly, "Anyway we're not old enough. So what can we do?"

Mopsy thought hard for a long time. Then she said, "We'll have to do something that helps people, something that people don't like doing much..."

"Like sweeping, polishing, dusting and cleaning," said Michael, who had heard his mother complaining about all the work she had to do each day.

"That's just what I mean," said Mopsy. "We can offer ourselves as home helps! We'll do the dusting and cleaning on Saturdays when we don't go to school..."

Michael didn't really like the sound of that but he had to agree that it was a good idea. So that very Saturday they went to their Aunty Margaret's house and offered themselves as home helps. "I shall be delighted to employ you both," said Aunty Margaret, and she gave them lots of dusting and polishing to do. Then, after a very nice tea, she told them to clear away all the dishes and fold the tablecloth.

At the end of the afternoon Mopsy and Michael were tired out. They were very happy, though, for they had earned enough to buy their mother two lovely birthday presents!

A Day Off

"Whose idea was it to clean windows for a living?" groaned Chuck Chimp.

"It was *your* idea," replied his pals, Chick and Chip.

"Well my arms are killing me," moaned Chuck. "Rub, rub. Polish, polish. Up and down those ladders all day."

"But it keeps you fit," chorused Chick and Chip.

"Fit to drop," groaned Chuck Chimp.

"Okay," said Chick to Chuck. "Tomorrow you can have a day off. Chip will drive the truck and I'll clean the windows. You just come along for the ride."

"Great!" beamed Chuck.

Next day Chip drove the truck, and Chick did all the work. Chick was exhausted but Chuck was so happy he began to sing and dance in the back of the truck.

The Firework

Podgy Pig was enjoying a sandwich when Ron Rabbit knocked at his door. "Come quickly, Podgy!" called Ron. "Timmy Mouse has found a huge firework in the field and he's going to let it off in five minutes."

"Five minutes?" mumbled Podgy Pig. "That should just give me time to do something important first."

"What's that?" asked Ron.

"Finish my banana sandwich!" muttered Podgy, seriously.

When Podgy and Ron arrived in the field they saw Timmy Mouse was about to set light to the touch-paper of the rocket. "Stand back!" squealed Timmy. "Please stand *back!*"

"Why should we stand back?" snorted Podgy.

Just as he spoke there was a huge *whoosh!* The rocket took off, giving Podgy a really nasty fright.

"Oh dear. Now I know why we should stand well clear of fireworks!" gasped Podgy. "I'll remember next time."

Wise Old Owl

If we were very quiet and tip-toed softly through the wood on a very dark night, we might find Wise Old Owl at home.

In the darkness we might see a soft light shining out of a hollow tree. If we could just peep inside the tree, this is what we would see: Wise Old Owl wearing his woolly hat and sitting in his favourite armchair, reading his book by the light of a candle.

And on a little shelf beside Wise Old Owl would be the owl's little friend, Sigmund Mouse; snoozing as usual.

Bonzo's Ball

Bonzo liked to chase the rabbits across Bunny Meadow. It was his favourite game. But the rabbits of Bunny Meadow soon grew fed up with Bonzo. They liked to nibble the grass in peace, and they didn't like Bonzo chasing them.

One day the chief rabbit had an idea. He gave Bonzo a coloured ball to play with. Bonzo was very pleased!

Now Bonzo chases the rubber ball instead of the rabbits of Bunny Meadow.

Flying Mice

Tiny and Tubby wanted to do some hang-gliding . . . but how? Tiny Mouse put his thinking-cap on and came up with an idea.

Later, Tiny and Tubby Mouse crept through the undergrowth near the big ponds.

"S-sh!" cried Tiny. "Don't make a sound!"

"I'm not. I never even squeaked," said Tubby.

They moved forward, whiskers twitching; and stopped.

"There it is!" said Tiny, pointing. A big sign read: Toodlepop Pond. "Now we want to find the bird," he said.

The big white bird was a stork, and it slept on the bank of the pond.

"P-sst!" said Tiny in the stork's ear. "Will you take us hang-gliding on Big Hill, please?"

"Of course," said the stork. "But how will you hang on once we're in the air?"

"We've brought our safety belts," squeaked Tiny. "I'll tie myself to your left foot, and Tubby will tie himself to your right foot."

Soon they were ready for take-off. Five minutes later they were flying high over the Big Hill.

The Happy Pilot

Barney Bear was on his way to collect his week's supply of honey. As he passed Three Acre Field he saw a rusty old aeroplane by the hedge. A sign hanging from its broken wing said: Anyone who would like this aeroplane may have it.

Barney had always wanted to fly like his friend Buzzy Bee! He hired a truck and took the aeroplane home; he cleaned off the rust, mended the engine and fitted new wings. Barney was very pleased when, after many weeks' hard work, his new plane was ready to try.

Buzzy Bee brought him an umbrella, which Barney fixed behind the cockpit. "You can use the umbrella as a parachute in case anything goes wrong," chuckled Buzzy.

On the day Barney tried his first flight all the animals came out to cheer. The little plane's wings rattled and the engine made a strange noise... but Barney was flying!

Now Barney Bear and Buzzy Bee can do both the things they enjoy together: eating honey *and* flying!

Sid and the Banana

Sid the Ant was just about to sit down on a twig – when he saw something long and yellow lying in the grass.

At first, Sid the Ant couldn't make out what it was. But when he came closer he saw that it was a banana.

"Someone has dropped a banana in the grass!" chirped Sid. "And it's ages since I've had a go on a banana slide!"

So all afternoon Sid had great fun, climbing to the top of the banana and sliding down again.

Feeding the Ducks

Sam Bear and his mother liked to go and feed the ducks in the park. Mum would save some scraps of bread and put them in a special bag marked DUCKS.

After shopping, Sam and his mum would take the bag of duck food down off the shelf and go out to the pond in the park.

One of the ducks had some babies and Sam and his mother liked to be sure that the ducklings had plenty of bread to eat so they would grow big and strong.

67

A Fair Deal

Rob the Red Squirrel was sitting under a chestnut tree brushing his tail. The grass was soft, the sun was warm and there were fruit and nuts in the trees. Rob was a happy squirrel – until George the Grey Squirrel came rushing by.

"Oh dear," muttered George the Grey Squirrel. "If ony I could go to the fair."

"Why shouldn't you go to the fair?" asked Rob.

"Because I can't afford to buy a ticket," sighed George.

"Let me think a moment," said Rob the Red Squirrel, scratching his head. At that very moment a chestnut fell off the tree above them.

"There's your answer!" cried Rob. "You can collect a mixture of nuts, put them in a barrow, and sell them for a penny each. I'll help you if you like."

"Great! Then I'll be able to buy a ticket," cried George with delight.

"Two tickets please, George," laughed Rob. "Because I'd like to go to the fair with you!"

The Treasure Map

Pirate Pete of Peckham found a treasure map in his Great-uncle Sam's sea chest. "This looks *very* interesting!" said Pirate Pete. "But it will cost me a fortune to hire a ship and reach the treasure island."

Pirate Pete turned to his parrot, which was called Polly, and said, "What do you say, Polly?"

"Pretty Polly," croaked Polly.

"That settles it!" cried Pete. "We sail as soon as we can find a ship!"

So Pete, with Polly on his shoulder, found a ship and filled it full of pirate food and parrot food and sailed to the little island in the middle of the big blue sea.

Pirate Pete, guided by the treasure map, dug a deep hole and soon found a treasure chest buried there. But when he opened up the treasure chest, there was nothing inside except a note which read: *If anyone finds this treasure chest please return it to Great-uncle Sam, care of Pirate Pete of Peckham.*

"Quaarrk!" cried Polly.

Horace the Hamster

Old Horace the Hamster had driven his steamroller for twenty-five happy years. Everybody knew and loved old Horace. Even the trees smiled when they saw Horace the Hamster and his steamroller come rolling by.

One day Horace was sent a pocket-watch by the mayor. The old hamster was very proud of it and kept it in the top pocket of his overalls.

When Horace heard that the mayor was coming to meet him, he was the happiest hamster in the land. And, as he wanted to look his best, he decided to give his overalls a press. Horace laid cardboard under the overalls and drove the steamroller over them. He did it very carefully so that the creases were all in the right places.

But *crunch!* Poor Horace had forgotten to take out his pocket-watch! Luckily for Horace, the mayor heard about the accident. When he met Horace, he gave him a new pocket-watch, this time made of gold!

Sam Scare-Nobody

Sam the Scarecrow stood in the middle of the big field and looked very sad. The farmer had put him there to scare away the crows and the moles and the rabbits. But no one seemed to be scared of Sam the Scarecrow. And it made him feel such a failure.

"What should I do?" moaned Sam. "I'm no good at all as a scarecrow. Perhaps I should get a job as a clown instead."

"Please don't be sad," said Rosie the Rabbit. "All the animals love you very much. *We* don't want you to be a scary scarecrow. We want you to stay as nice a scarecrow as you are."

"That's right!" agreed Marcus the Mole. "All the animals think you're a very nice scarecrow."

"And here!" added Rosie the Rabbit. "We've brought you some flowers to cheer you up."

"Thank you," said Sam. "And you have cheered me up. Because I don't really *want* to be a scary scarecrow."

Fox in a Fix

Roger the Rabbit and Rob the Red Squirrel both knew a cosy hollow where they could lie down and snooze in the sunshine. It was full of soft green grass and buttercups. Because it was their favourite place, Roger and Rob had hidden some carrots and acorns there in an oak tree larder.

When Ferdy the Fox heard about this he hid in a tree and waited for the two friends to come along. But both Roger and Rob had keen eyesight and they saw Ferdy the Fox long before he saw them. So, instead of leading Ferdy to their oak tree larder, they led him into the back garden of their friend Joe Bear, who chased the fox away with a growl.

Lily Lake

Baby Beaver and Betsy Beaver were walking home along the banks of Lily Lake, when suddenly the sun came out.

"Gosh!" said Betsy Beaver. "That sunshine is so nice and warm. And look, Baby Beaver, see how it makes the water of Lily Lake shine like silver."

"It's beautiful!" chirped Baby Beaver. "But why is it called Lily Lake?"

"Because of the water-lilies," replied Betsy Beaver. "Come along and I'll show you."

Betsy sat little Baby Beaver on a log and paddled out into the water until they reached the water-lilies.

"Water-lilies are really beautiful," chirped Baby Beaver, as he swam in the water. "I think Lily Lake is my favourite place!"

Bingo's Dreams

Bingo the Dog liked to lie in front of the fire. It was his favourite place.

Once Bingo had settled down it didn't take long for him to go to sleep. When he was asleep, Bingo would often dream. Sometimes he would dream he was chasing rabbits across a big wide meadow.

Bingo usually felt very tired after chasing those dream rabbits. So when he awoke he was always pleased to find himself back home, beside a nice warm fire, lying on his favourite rug.

Charlie's House

Charlie Rabbit had moved away from Whitetail Warren over a year ago. All the rabbits missed him, but his best friend Rocky missed him more than anyone.

One day the postman brought Rocky a letter from his old friend Charlie. Rocky was very excited and read the letter to his family.

Charlie's letter was full of news about his home in Toadstool Wood, which had taken him a long time to find. It was a big, old toadstool in a quiet corner of the wood and Charlie had been very busy painting, mending and gardening – which is why he hadn't written to Rocky before!

Now the toadstool house looked neat and clean; there were juicy radishes and crisp lettuce in the garden...and Charlie had written specially to ask if Rocky would like to spend his holiday there. What do *you* think?

Thirsty Mouse

Melinda Mouse wanted a drink of orange juice. She went to the supermarket to buy some but they didn't have any mouse-sized cartons.

Luckily, Melinda had a friend called Frank who had an ice-cream and soft drinks shop. So Melinda went to see him. "I'd like some orange juice, please, Frank," she squeaked.

Frank poured her a glass and put a straw in it. Then he put a toy ladder up against the glass. Melinda climbed up the ladder and had a nice refreshing drink through the straw.

Circus Elephant

Jubbly the Circus Elephant plodded down the ramp of the jumbo jet with his suitcase in his trunk. (He'd been back to the jungle on holiday.)

Ahead he saw a big sign which read: Circus Elephants This Way.

"That's me," he smiled to himself, and followed the sign.

After Jubbly had eaten a huge plate full of circus elephant buns, he called in to see the circus ring-master.

"Hello, Jubbly. Welcome back!" greeted the circus ring-master. "Did you enjoy your holidays?"

"Great!" said Jubbly. "And what's more I was taught a few more circus tricks by my pals in the jungle!"

75

Snow Games

One winter morning when the animals awoke they found their hillside covered in a thick blanket of snow. Everyone was very excited. As it was Saturday no one had to go to school, so there would be plenty of time to play.

Patrick Pig was the first to finish breakfast – of course! He began building a snowman, patting the soft snow into shape with his mittens. Fonzo Fox thought a giant snowball would be fun...until it rolled over him and took him off down the hill! The little foxes had a snowball fight, while Rusty the Cat and Patrick's brother, Percy, tried skiing for the first time. The rabbit family had two sledges – a big one and a little one.

Someone else in the picture has an even smaller sledge: can you find it?

Perhaps it would have been better if the animals had found bigger spaces for their games!

76

Greengrocer Bob

Ever since he was a small bear, Bob had always wanted to become a greengrocer. "It would be good to sell really fresh vegetables to all my animal friends," he said.

When he grew up, Bob Bear worked very hard to make his dream come true. He rented a small plot of land from Farmer Fox. After clearing the weeds, Bob prepared the soil carefully and sowed lots of seeds. He watered and weeded all summer and when autumn came Bob harvested many vegetables. There were carrots, marrows, onions, potatoes and lots more.

Bob filled his wooden wheelbarrow with the newly-picked vegetables and wheeled it into the woods to deliver them to his friends. Some of the animals thought they might not like vegetables, but once they had tried them they asked Bob Bear to bring his wheelbarrow every week. Now he has many happy – and healthy – customers.

Coco the Clown

Coco the Clown sat down in the middle of the circus ring and began to cry. No one knew what was wrong.

The trapeze artist went to tell the ring master, and the ring master went to tell Colin the Clown, who was Coco's best friend.

When they found that Coco was still crying the ring master didn't know what to say so he asked Colin the Clown to talk to Coco.

"What is wrong, Coco?" asked Colin. "Why are you crying?"

"I'm so sad because everyone keeps laughing at me," replied Coco.

"But people laugh at you because you're a good clown," said Colin. "That should make you *happy*!"

"I suppose so," sniffed Coco. "But I do wish clowns didn't have to be funny *all* the time. Just once in a while I'd like to be a really *sad* clown. Then, when I've made people feel very sad – I could cheer them up again!"

The Twins

Billy and Willie Bear were twins. They wore the same clothes and smiled the same smiles.

If Willie scratched his head, Billy would scratch his head as well!

When Billy whistled a tune, Willie would whistle it too.

At their birthday party, after a lovely tea, they entertained their parents and friends with some jokes, funny dancing and some acrobatics. They kept together perfectly.

"You are twice as good as I expected!" said their proud father.

Sybil's Favourite Song

Sybil was a beautiful white swan who lived on a woodland lake. She looked so graceful as she floated on the smooth waters.

Jack the Rabbit liked to stand on the shore and watch Sybil pass by.

One day he thought he heard Sybil singing. But when she came closer Jack was amazed to see Betty the Bluebird perched on Sybil's back.

It was Betty who was singing, and Sybil was listening to every note. After all, it was her favourite tune.

79

The Sound of Music

Once upon a time, Harry Hippo decided he could sing. Of course he couldn't *really* sing. But no one dared tell him. Because Harry was so sure he could sing, he called a few of his friends together for a sing-song.

Crocodile came. (He couldn't sing either.) Lion came. (He was Harry's best friend.) Two monkeys and two tortoises came (but they turned up by chance). Finally Crazy Crow, with a stripy beak, arrived.

"Right!" said Harry Hippo. "What shall we sing?"

"What about 'Three Blind Mice'?" suggested Crocodile.

"I don't know that one," cawed Crazy Crow. "But as it's my birthday . . ."

"Happy birthday to you," sang Harry Hippo and his friends.

"Oh! What a terrible noise!" thought Crazy Crow as he flapped away. "Harry Hippo really ought to take some singing lessons!"

Hippos in the Snow

Beefy and Tubby, the hippopotamus brothers, were looking through their bedroom window. They were pleased to see that more snow had fallen in the night.

After breakfast, Beefy and Tubby ran out into the snow-covered garden. Beefy threw a snowball at Tubby – which knocked his hat off! Tubby wasn't fast enough to throw his snowball at Beefy, who hid behind a tree!

"This snow is cold," said Beefy. "My hippo toes are frozen!"

"Let's do something to keep us warm," suggested Tubby. "Let's make a snowman."

"I'd rather make a snow*hippo!*" laughed Beefy.

By the time they had finished they were feeling warm and happy ... and the snowhippo was looking quite pleased with itself, too!

Mr and Mrs Chimp

"Let's do as the humans do," suggested Mrs Chimp.

"Do you mean sit in front of the television all day?" asked Mr Chimp.

"No," said Mrs Chimp. "I mean let's have a nice cup of tea and some cakes."

"Okay," said Mr Chimp. "I'll try it this once."

Mr Chimp watched as Mrs Chimp put on her apron and laid the tea-table. He continued to watch as Mrs Chimp toasted some muffins.

Then Mrs Chimp made a pot of tea and gave Mr Chimp a cup and saucer to hold in his hand.

"Put the cup on my head," said Mr Chimp. "I don't want to be mistaken for one of those humans."

Billy the Baker

Billy the Rabbit was a baker. He made different kinds of cakes and bread and carried them around in a basket. He'd shout, "Cakes for sale. Five pence each. Buns for sale. Four pence each. Bread for sale – ten pence a loaf!"

Billy made some lovely cakes and he always had lots of customers.

One person who always bought a cake from Billy the Rabbit was Mrs Tipple, who lived at the top of a very tall house.

One day Mrs Tipple wasn't feeling very well and so she couldn't come down to buy her usual cake from Billy the baker. So Mrs Tipple asked a songbird to go down and collect her cake from Billy.

Billy gave the songbird Mrs Tipple's cake and said, "Little songbird, if you come and see me when I've sold all my cakes, you can have all the crumbs you want from the bottom of my basket."

Uncle Ned's Present

One morning Charlie Chimp found a huge parcel on his front doorstep. Charlie was very surprised, as it wasn't his birthday and Christmas was a long way off. A label on the parcel read: *To Charlie Chimp, from Uncle Ned.*

Charlie tried to move Uncle Ned's parcel, but it was so heavy he could only lift one end! Charlie needed help, so he went next door to see his friend Pinky Pig.

"Please will you help me lift my parcel indoors, Pinky?" asked Charlie.

After a great struggle Charlie and Pinky managed to lift the funny-shaped parcel... but it was too big to fit through Charlie's front door! Finally Charlie and Pinky moved the parcel onto the lawn and unwrapped it. Inside was a piano!

"But you can't play a piano!" laughed Pinky.

"Neither can Uncle Ned," said Charlie. "I think that's why he sent it to me!"

Sausage Dog

Six days a week Bob the Dog had tinned dogfood mixed with biscuit for his dinner, which he enjoyed, but for a special treat every Wednesday Bob was given sausages! Sausages were definitely Bob's favourite food.

One fine Wednesday afternoon Bob was relaxing in his kennel. The butcher had just delivered his sausages, the sun was warm and Bob was thinking about the big bone he had just buried under the oak tree at the bottom of the garden.

Suddenly, his sausages began to move!

"I must be dreaming," thought Bob. But no, sure enough, the sausages were slowly moving out of his dog-bowl!

"Oops! Sorry, Bob!" squeaked Sydney Squirrel. "I was trying to prove to Sam Squirrel here that he needn't be afraid of your sausages."

"Why should anyone be afraid of sausages?" laughed Bob.

"Because Sam thought your string of sausages was a funny-shaped snake!" giggled Sydney.

Pixie Paula

Paula was a pixie who lived in a pixie house in a peaceful part of the wood. Paula loved music. She could sing beautiful songs with her soft pixie voice all day long, and often entertained her friends who lived in the wood.

One day her grandfather gave her a pixie flute made out of the wood of an old plum tree.

Paula tried to play her flute amongst trees and the woodland flowers. The sound of her playing made the wood mice and other friends come out to see what the strange noise was. It was some time before everyone agreed that Paula's present had been a good idea!

The Ant's Paradise

"I'll find myself a nice flower," thought Arthur Ant, "and I'll climb to the top and see what's going on up there."

So Arthur Ant walked on until he came to the base of a flower. "Here goes!" said Arthur as he began to climb the stem of the flower.

It was a tall flower, and Arthur needed to rest on a leaf before he reached the top. Up, up, he climbed, higher and higher, until he was above the tallest blade of grass.

Finally, Arthur Ant climbed into the heart of a cup-shaped flower and stood gazing at the pool of rain which had collected there.

"I've always wanted a paddling pool!" laughed Arthur.

Wishing-Well Hill

John and Mary were staying at their Uncle Ben's. One day Uncle Ben took them out into the countryside in his car. He took them to a lovely place full of winding roads and rolling hills.

One of the hills was called Wishing-well Hill, because on the top of the hill was an old wishing-well. Uncle Ben parked his car at the bottom of the hill and let John and Mary climb up to the top to see the wishing-well.

When John and Mary reached the wishing-well they found lots of beautiful flowers growing around it.

John didn't really know what to wish for, but then he remembered that Mary wanted a pet rabbit for her birthday, so he wished for that.

A little rabbit hiding at the other side of the well heard John's wish and hopped out!

Knights of the Round Table

Toby the Tortoise has always been interested in
stories of King Arthur and his Knights of the
Round Table. One day Roger the Rabbit and Rob
the Red Squirrel came to visit Toby. After having
some beans on toast together, Toby told his friends he'd like to play a
special game. He called it Knights of the Round Tortoise.

"Sir Roger Rabbit can ride on my back," said Toby.

"And I'll be Sir Rob Red Squirrel," chirped Rob.

The three friends had great fun together. They used dustbin lids for
shields. Roger the Rabbit made himself a boxing-glove lance. And Toby
charged along at twice his normal speed.

Funfair

The funfair was in full swing. The roundabout was going around. The big wheel was turning. The sun was shining. Lots of people and animals were enjoying themselves.

Little Elsie could see it all from her bedroom window. But she couldn't go to the funfair, because she was poorly, and had to stay in bed. She had her books and her dolls and her paints and her modelling clay, but she would rather have been at the funfair.

Later that day she had a visitor. It was her Uncle Ben. Her Uncle Ben had come specially to see her.

"Oh, I do wish I could go the funfair Uncle Ben," said Elsie.

"Well," suggested Uncle Ben. "Why not use your modelling clay and your dolls and your toys and your paints and have your own funfair – right here in your bedroom?"

So Elsie did just that! She imagined she was at her own funfair. And one by one all her favourite toys came to join in the fun.

The Giant

Mrs Miller lived in a windmill in the village of Thimbledown. When the wind blew, it turned the sails of the windmill. When the sails moved they turned the millstones, which ground the corn to make the bread.

One sad day the windmill broke down and Mrs Miller couldn't make any more bread.

Now a giant with a huge club had been seen on the outskirts of Thimbledown village. Everybody locked their doors and hid in fear. All except Mrs Miller, who took her broom and went out to meet him.

She found him standing at the edge of the wood looking for food.

"How would you like some bread to eat?" asked Mrs Miller.

"Yum yum. Sounds good!" boomed the giant.

"Well, if you come back to the windmill with me you can grind lots of corn with that club of yours. Then I'll bake you all the bread you want."

"Yummy!" said the giant, later on. "I've not tasted bread so good since I was a small boy."

The Friendly Rabbits

Raymond, Roger and Ruth Rabbit were the best of friends. They liked to meet in the playground and play games together.

Ruth had a red hoop which she used as a *hula* hoop. She also liked to roll her red hoop along the ground and chase after it.

Roger had a big striped ball which he would throw into the air and try to catch. When he got tired of this he would play football.

Raymond had a bat and ball. Raymond liked to see how many times he could hit the ball into the air with his bat.

Sometimes the friendly rabbits would share each other's toys, and think up new games to play with them.

Paddle Boat

The two young hippos, Beefy and Tubby, were on their way to the park. They had a new toy boat and wanted to try it on the pond there.

"While we sail our new boat we can have a paddle in the water at the same time," suggested Tubby.

"I don't feel like getting my feet wet today. I'd rather just float the boat from the bank," said Beefy.

Beefy and Tubby pushed their toy boat carefully out into the water. It sailed beautifully, right out to the middle of the pond... and then stopped!

"Oh dear, it's stuck!" said Tubby. "What shall we do now?"

"Well, as you wanted to go for a paddle, why not climb into the water now and rescue our boat?" suggested Beefy.

Tubby took off his shoes and rolled up his trousers before stepping into the cold pond-water, but the hippos hadn't realised how deep it was! When Tubby reached the boat only his head showed above the water – and a seagull perched on it! Beefy thought his brother looked so silly he took a picture of him!

Picnic in the Sun

"This is perfect for a picnic!" cried Sam Spaniel. "I'll ask Mum to pack me a hamper, then I'll go off to the meadow and have a picnic in the sun!

"Why not take your friend Marion Mouse with you to the meadow?" suggested Mum.

"Good idea, Mum!" said Sam. "I'll carry her in the hamper."

When Sam opened up the hamper in the meadow the first thing he did was to have a nice drink of orange juice. Marion Mouse nibbled at a sandwich and cried: "Oh! Cheese sandwich! My favourite!"

Rainbow Treasure

Maurice Mole could see the end of the rainbow ahead of him.

"Everybody knows there's a pot of gold at the end of the rainbow," gasped Maurice. "If I hurry along I might find it."

Maurice scampered along, running as fast as his legs could carry him. Suddenly he found himself standing right under the end of the rainbow.

The colours were marvellous! Maurice had never seen anything so beautiful in all his life.

In fact, he was so delighted that he forgot all about looking for the pot of gold!

92

Sweetflower Meadow

It was such a warm sunny day that Aunty Alice Rabbit and her nephew Robin Rabbit had gone out walking. They had only gone a few metres when Robin Rabbit suddenly said, "Please, Aunty Alice, can we go to Sweetflower Meadow?"

"Of course we can," replied Aunty Alice. "But why do you want to go there, Robin?"

"Well," said Robin, "there is someone waiting at Sweetflower Meadow who would like to see you; but I can't tell you who it is because it's supposed to be a big secret . . ." As the two rabbits walked through the bright sunshine Aunty Alice wondered who it could be.

When they arrived at the edge of the meadow the two rabbits were met by Bob the Dog.

"Hello, Aunty Alice!" greeted Bob. "I just wanted to give you these presents from my children."

"Good gracious me!" gasped Aunty Alice. "Why have you brought presents for me, Bob? It's not my birthday."

"I know that," beamed Bob, "but often in the past you have given my children little gifts. So we all decided that *you* should have some presents for a change."

"Well, bless you," cried Aunty Alice. "This is a wonderful surprise!"

Flying Laundry

It was a damp day with no wind and Mrs Helen Hare had washed some clothes. At breakfast time she hung them on the line with wooden clothes-pegs and waited for them to dry.

After she had made lunch for her husband Hubert Hare and herself, Helen checked the clothes on the line. Everything was still as wet as it had been at breakfast time!

"That's because it is such a damp day, with no wind," explained Hubert. "What we need is a really good, strong breeze to blow the clothes dry."

"Can you think of a way to make the wind blow the washing dry?" asked his wife.

"I could tie the clothes-line to the back of my red aeroplane," said Hubert, helpfully. "Then, when I'm flying through the air, the clothes should soon dry." Soon Hubert took off in his shiny red aeroplane – with the clothes-line tied to the back!

The local animals were astonished to see Hubert and his plane up high in the sky with a line of washing trailing behind him. But his wife was very pleased when he landed with all the family's washing dry and ready to iron!

The Snail and the Tortoise

Seb the Snail and Stan the Tortoise liked to go for walks together. They travelled very slowly but that didn't stop them enjoying themselves.

They both knew every blade of grass in the garden where they lived. And no matter how far they walked, they only had to pop their heads under their shells to be back home again!

The Clockwork Carrot

Tufty the Rabbit had been given lots of presents at Christmas; a pair of rabbit socks from Aunty Bunny, a rabbit handkerchief from Great Aunt Bunny and a rabbit tie from Grandma Bunny.

Tufty opened another present and found a nice orange carrot inside. But when Tufty put it on the floor, the carrot began to jump and wriggle across the room!

"It's alive!" gasped Tufty, but then he realised that it was a *clockwork* carrot!

"I'll take it to school with me," he said. "And I'll show it to all my friends. Perhaps they'll think it's alive too!"

The Gang

One day after school, Kenneth, Buster, Jimmy and Skinny went for a walk to a piece of waste ground. There they stopped and had a pow-wow.

"I'm fat, I know," said Skinny. "But I'm tired of being teased."

"And I'm just the opposite," said Kenneth, who was the tallest of the friends. "And I'm tired of being bullied."

"So am I," said Buster and Jimmy together.

"We'll have to turn ourselves into a gang," said Skinny. "We'll call ourselves the Bulldogs!"

"We don't look like a gang," said Jimmy.

"We can change that," said Kenneth. "Let's look around and see what we can find to make us look frightening,"

The four friends spent the next hour searching around the waste ground and found lots of things to make them look different. When they were satisfied that they looked fierce enough they marched back to the school where some of the biggest bullies were playing bat-and-ball, and challenged them to a fight. But the gang's strange appearance gave the bullies such a shock that they ran away!

The Bulldogs are very popular in the district. Nobody dares challenge them and now lots of boys want to join their gang. So far, however, the Bulldogs won't let them!

The Absent-Minded Professor

There was once a very absent-minded Professor. When he was younger he built his own house but forgot that he had made a front door. The next day he made another door, so his new house had two front doors.

Sometimes the Professor went for a walk. As soon as he had left by one front door he forgot why he was outside, and went back inside almost at once by means of his second door.

The Professor's wife loved him very much but she was often cross with him because he forgot so many things. "I will put a mat and a bowl of flowers beside the door that you should use," she said at last. "Then I will know when you are going out and coming in."

She did this the same day but the Professor soon forgot what he was supposed to do. He went on using both doors! At last his poor wife boarded up the second door and the Professor, no matter how hard he pushed, could never get it to move.

After a time he forgot there had been a door to push. Now, when he goes for a stroll, he uses the door with the big mat in front of it to get back into the house and that makes his wife very happy!

Frobisher Frog

Frobisher was a very naughty young frog. His brothers and sisters were all quite well-behaved and were seldom in trouble – but Frobisher was different.

When they were tadpoles in the big pond it was always Frobisher who got lost in the weed! As the young ones lost their tails and grew long back legs the parent frogs taught their children how to jump from the bank and plop into the shallow water. But Frobisher thought *he* knew everything and didn't listen to the lessons.

One day he found a lily leaf and climbed onto it. "How clever I am," he thought. But the silly frog didn't realise that the lily leaf was floating away from the bank and out into the middle of the pond. Frobisher was stuck! He felt very lonely and sad all by himself and wished after all he had learnt his jumping lessons.

When his father came to rescue him much later that day, Frobisher promised to pay attention in future... and he did.

Sarah

Sarah Rabbit loved to knit. She could knit scarves, hats, jumpers and woollen boots for any rabbit.

Sarah liked to use wool of many different colours. She had made a red scarf, a blue hat and a yellow jumper in only one week.

Next week she was going to knit a pair of mittens for herself. That was to stop her paws from getting cold in the winter. Because with warm paws, Sarah could knit lots of winter gifts for her rabbit friends.

Billy Bear

Billy Bear woke up on the first day of his holiday and stretched. "I'm going to spend today being very lazy," he decided.

The sun was shining and the air was warm. "Just right for sitting in the garden and reading my favourite book," said Billy

After breakfast Billy looked in the shed for his deckchair. It took him a long time to find out how to make it stand up! He then put a small table beside it, on which he stood a jar of special honey – just in case he got hungry before lunch! – and a glass of cool lemonade. The last thing Billy looked for was his sun-hat, which he only wore when he was on holiday.

Now everything was ready. Billy settled down to enjoy his book ... *Goldilocks and the Three Bears*. Have you read it?

Fluff's Adventure

Fluff the Dog woke up in his dog basket and yawned. "This kind of life is too easy," he sighed. "What I need is an adventure to stop me getting too fat." So Fluff padded outside into the garden and sniffed the air.

"I think I'll go through the garden gate," he said to himself. "And I'll follow the first thing I see. That should give me an adventure."

The first thing Fluff saw was an odd looking brown bird. So Fluff began to scamper after the bird. Wherever the bird went, Fluff followed. Through the grass. Past some flowers. Through more grass. Past some more flowers. Through even more grass.

After an hour of this Fluff was exhausted. But imagine his surprise when he turned around and saw he was only a short distance from his own back garden. The bird he'd been following had been flying around in circles!

"I'm glad I'm not far from home," sighed Fluff, "because I'm very hungry after my adventure."

I-Spy

Sheila and Carl were sitting on the lawn. They were playing a game called I-spy. Sheila said: "I spy with my little eye, something beginning with the letter C."

Now Carl had to guess what Sheila had seen... "Is it 'cat'?" asked Carl, because he could see the cat asleep on the fence. Sheila shook her head. "Is it 'car'?" asked Carl, looking at his toy car.

"No. It's not your car," said Sheila.

Carl looked around again. "Is it 'cloud'?" he asked. "Because if it isn't cloud, I don't know what it could be."

"No, it's not cloud," laughed Sheila. "I'll tell you what it is... It's *Carl*... I spied *you* with my little eye!"

The Three Pandas

The three pandas, wearing coloured waistcoats, trousers, and carrying umbrellas, were out walking.

"What a perfectly splendid day for a game of golf," said one. "Blue sky, gentle breeze."

"I thought only humans played golf," said the second panda.

"There's nothing to stop pandas playing golf," declared the first panda. "Nothing at all."

"Let's use our umbrellas as golf clubs," said the third panda. "And use a grapefruit as a golf ball."

All the pandas needed now were some holes in the ground, and after a little while they found one.

"This is how it should be done," said the third panda, who knocked his grapefruit straight down the hole.

The very next second a rabbit popped up out of the hole with a grapefruit balanced on its head. "Hey!" he said. "Please stop knocking your grapefruit down my rabbit hole!"

102

Wally Woodpecker

From early morning until late evening Wally Woodpecker's beak could be heard as it tapped in the tree tops of Happytree Forest.

Wally sometimes pecked holes in the tree trunks which other birds could use as a nest and this gave Ronald Rabbit a bright idea! He asked Wally to carve out numbers on some flat pieces of wood.

Wally soon went to work, pecking out the numbers for Ronald.

"We can hang the numbers on the tree next to our homes," said Ronald Rabbit to his friends. "That will make the postman's job so much easier!"

The Thirsty Plant

The sun had been shining all summer and Matt Mouse had spent his days playing golf. In the evening Matt liked to watch the television.

He loved to see the funny cartoons and tape them on his mouse video.

Although Matt enjoyed the hot, sunny weather he was hoping that it would rain soon because his pot plant was getting *very* thirsty.

One evening when Matt was watching television he heard the *plip plop* of raindrops falling on his rooftop.

"Yippee!" squeaked Matt. "Now I can treat my pot plant to its favourite drink!"

Toby's Portrait

Toby Tortoise had always wanted
his portrait painted, so when he
heard that Monsieur Pablo Squirrel, the famous
artist, was in town, he went to see him.

"Monsieur Pablo," said Toby, "please will you
paint my portrait?"

"But of course, Monsieur Toby," replied Pablo. "My fee is
three beech-nuts and an acorn for a water-colour and six
hazelnuts for an oil-painting."

Toby had saved enough hazelnuts and decided on an oil-
painting. "I'd like to wear my top hat for the picture," he said.

"That will look very grand, Monsieur Toby," agreed Pablo. "I will come to
your house next Tuesday with my brushes and paints."

Toby had to sit very still while Monsieur Pablo worked. When the
portrait was finished Toby was so pleased he gave the artist an extra
hazelnut – *and* his top hat!

The Happy Clown

Colin the Clown worked at the local circus. Every night he made people laugh. During the day Colin often went for a walk in the woods.

The animals knew when Colin was in the woods because he would whistle a special tune as he strolled along.

Colin loved walking in the woods. He knew the names of all the birds and the trees and flowers. In his pocket Colin would carry scraps of bread and nuts to feed the animals and birds in the woods . . .

He would give nuts to the squirrels and mice, and crumbs to the birds. Colin the Clown didn't make the animals and birds laugh, but he always made them happy.

Jimbo and Pedro

Jimbo the Elephant was bored. So he went to see his friend Pedro the Panda.

"Oh dear. I'm so terribly bored!" he said to Pedro.

"Bored? How can you possibly be bored?" asked Pedro the Panda. "I'm always so busy *doing* things."

"What kind of things?" yawned Jimbo the Elephant.

"Watching the stars. Reading story-books. Eating sandwiches. Playing on the banana slide."

"A banana slide!" cried Jimbo, pricking up his ears. "That sounds like fun."

"It is fun!" laughed Pedro. "Why not come along to the banana slide now?"

So Pedro and Jimbo played on the banana slide for hours. Jimbo enjoyed himself so much he wondered how he could *ever* have been bored!

Scamp's Bone

It was a hot day and Scamp the Dog was burying a bone in the garden. As he did so, he saw that the soil was very dry.

"This soil is as dry as a bone," he quipped to himself. So he picked up the hose pipe and turned on the water. (He wanted to give the flowers a refreshing drink.)

Later, after Scamp had watered the flowers, he realised he was hungry. So he had to dig up his bone again!

106

The Two Bears

The two bears were hungry. They had heard about a very mean old bear who sometimes needed help with small jobs in his garden. They knocked on his door nervously and offered to work in return for honey.

"Honey, is it?" said the miserly old bear. "There's a big barrel of honey at the bottom of the well in my garden. If you clear out all the rubbish that is blocking the well you may have the honey."

The little bears rushed to the overgrown garden and began busily clearing the rubbish from the well.

"Silly bears," whispered the miser. "There's no honey in that well...just lots and lots of rubbish."

However, an hour later the small bears returned to the house looking very pleased with themselves. They had a wheelbarrow *full* of barrels! There was enough honey for two weeks!

It must have been a wishing-well!

Pen Pals

Tiddles Cat and Kitty Cat were pen pals. Tiddles lived in Ireland and Kitty lived in Switzerland, and they both enjoyed writing letters to each other.

When Kitty wrote and told Tiddles that she had been out tobogganing in the snow, Tiddles wrote straight back and said:

"I'd love to visit you one day, Kitty, and then perhaps we could go tobogganing together."

The next letter Tiddles received was from Kitty and with it was an airline ticket to Switzerland.

Tiddles packed her woollen scarf and hat, and flew off to Switzerland. On the day she arrived Kitty took her out tobogganing.

"This is great fun!" cried Tiddles as the toboggan whizzed along through the snow.

"When you're tired, Tiddles, we can go home and have some milk and a nice slice of Swiss roll for tea," said Kitty.

Kim the Koala Bear

As Kim the Koala Bear walked through the quiet woods, he saw a hollow log lying on the ground. "This looks like a good place to hide my jar of honey. But maybe I can find somewhere better. What should I do?" he said.

Kim the Koala Bear saw a flower on the ground. He picked the flower and pulled off a petal. "Shall I hide my honey here?" he wondered. Then he pulled off another petal. "Or shan't I . . . ?"

Buzby the Bee came along and when he saw Kim pulling the petals off the flower he landed on Kim's paw.

"Please don't do that, Kim," pleaded Buzby the Bee. "Because if you pick the flowers and pull the petals off them, the bees won't be able to make any more honey for you."

The Three Cycles

Rory Rabbit had a friend called Marty Mouse. Rory had a two-wheeled bicycle and Marty had a three-wheeled tricycle.

One day they rode into the country on their cycles. As they pedalled down a country lane they saw Bill Bear ahead. Bill was riding a great *big* bicycle. When Bill Bear saw Rory Rabbit and Marty Mouse, he stopped his bicycle and waited for them to catch up.

"Why don't we ride along together?" said Bill Bear. Rory Rabbit and Marty Mouse agreed. So Bill went first, followed by Rory and then Marty.

"You'd better make the hand signals Bill," squeaked Marty. "Because no one will see *my* signals!"

The Kind Robin

It was a very cold winter's day and the wind made all the grass shiver. A little robin was flying around looking for food to eat when he saw a caterpillar on a branch.

The caterpillar looked so cold and so sad that the robin took off his scarf and wrapped it around the caterpillar to keep it warm.

"Thank you very much!" said the caterpillar. "I've never felt so cold in all my life! But I feel much warmer now!"

"I'll find you a nice leaf to hide under now," said the robin. "And there you can sleep until summer comes with its warm sunshine."

Winter Flowers

Pete the Pixie was walking through the wood looking sadly at the bare branches and the brown earth. The birds had all flown south to spend the winter in a warm place, and the woodland creatures were busy preparing cosy nests.

"Oh, I do wish it was summer again," sighed Pete.

Suddenly, Pete had a wonderful idea. He sat down with coloured paper and pixie scissors and made lots of colourful paper flowers and leaves!

Later Pete went back to the wood and fixed the paper leaves and flowers to the bare trees. Then they looked just as bright and lovely as they did on a summer's day – and Pete the Pixie could enjoy his winter flowers until the real ones grew again.

111

The Bird House

Jimmy had a paper round. He was out in all kinds of weather delivering newspapers. Sometimes the sun was shining and he enjoyed himself. Other times the wind was blowing and once it was snowing. But Jimmy was a brave boy and didn't let the weather stop him delivering his papers.

Every week Jimmy gave some of the money he earned to his mother. Jimmy also saved some of the money to buy his sister a birthday present.

Jimmy's sister was called Jenny, and she loved to see the birds in the garden. She would watch them from the living-room window. There was one little blue bird she liked very much.

When Jenny's birthday came, Jimmy bought her a bird house. Jenny was very pleased.

Not long after her birthday, her favourite blue bird came and lived in the bird house in the garden. It was a birthday present which gave the whole family pleasure right through the year.

Strawberry Hill

Farmer Bear and Mrs Bear had a nice cosy farm which lay in the middle of two hills. On one side was Primrose Hill and on the other side was Strawberry Hill.

Mrs Bear had some nice hens which liked to peck for wild corn on Strawberry Hill. In the evening the hens would return to the hen hutch in the farmyard to roost.

One day Mrs Bear said to Farmer Bear, "My hens aren't laying many eggs for some reason."

"Leave it to me," said Farmer Bear. "I'll see if I can find out why."

Farmer Bear soon found out why! Porky Pig and Fudgie Fieldmouse were having go-kart races down Strawberry Hill and they were frightening Mrs Bear's nice hens.

"Would you please take your go-karts onto Primrose Hill?" asked Farmer Bear. "Then you won't disturb our hens."

"Okay," chorused Porky and Fudgie, and they drove off to race on Primrose Hill.

Moonlight Serenade

Cindy Cat was sitting up in bed and reading a book. . . .

Cindy had spent a lovely day with her friend Colin Cat. First the two friends had gone roller-skating on the Pussyland Roller-skating Rink. When they grew tired of roller-skating, Colin took Cindy to the cinema to see a film about a *gigantic* mouse who chased every cat he saw! Finally Colin and Cindy had left their roller-skates in Cindy's front room and had gone for a stroll underneath the stars.

Now Cindy was just settling down to sleep when she heard someone playing a guitar and singing in her garden!

"Who can that be I wonder?" whispered Cindy to herself. Cindy got out of bed and went to the window. Looking down she saw that it was Colin Cat and he was playing his guitar by the light of the moon.

"I left my roller-skates in your kitchen," explained Colin, "and I didn't want to wake you by knocking on the door. . . . So instead I sang to you!"

"Tomorrow I'd like to sing a duet with you," purred Cindy.

The Kangaroo Car

Fred and Mabel Fox had sold their bicycles and bought themselves a brand new sports car. It was called a kangaroo car.

"Why is it called a kangaroo car?" asked Mabel.

"I don't know," answered Fred. "But kangaroos move along at great speed. And that's just what we want to do in our new kangaroo car!"

So Fred and Mabel climbed into their new car and went for a drive into the country. At first Fred drove the kangaroo car very carefully. When they turned left, Mabel put out her hand to signal "left". And when they turned right, Fred put out his right hand to signal "right".

When at last they came to a long stretch of road Fred decided to go faster. But the moment the car went faster it began to bounce along.

"Oh no! This is terrible!" cried Fred. "The car is *bouncing* along like a kangaroo."

"I think I prefer my bicycle!" gasped Mabel.

King of the Jungle

Leo the Lion was prowling through the jungle. It had been raining earlier and now the dark green leaves were shiny and steam was rising from the jungle floor.

Leo's paws were covered in mud and his thick mane was tangled and untidy. Leo saw his reflection in a clear pool and was very ashamed.

"I'm the King of the Jungle," he sighed, "but I look far too scruffy for anyone to believe that!"

Leo threw back his huge head and gave a mighty roar. The ground shook and the trees rustled, so loud was the lion's voice.

In answer to his call four chattering monkeys swung down from a palm tree. "Yes, sir," said one, "what is your majesty's wish?"

"My muddy paws and tangled mane need grooming," roared Leo. "Please don't stop until my claws sparkle and my fur shines . . . and I once again look like a king!"

Woodland Games

Merry was a little fallow deer who liked to play in the woods. Merry had two friends called Flitter and Flutter. Flitter was a small butterfly and Flutter was a large butterfly.

The three of them would often play together. Their favourite game was hide and seek. The two butterflies would close their eyes and count to thirty while Merry ran off to hide amongst the trees.

Flitter and Flutter would then search for Merry. When they found her they'd both fly above her, fluttering their wings with delight.

Bill and Susie

Bill Bear's parents bought him a shiny mouth-organ for his birthday. It made a lovely sound and Bill practised very hard. Soon he was able to play nursery rhyme tunes on his mouth-organ.

Bill liked to practise in the little wood near his home, and the birds that lived there enjoyed listening to him. There was one bird called Susie who always flew down from the trees when Bill Bear played.

One day Susie asked Bill if she could sing the nursery rhyme words while he played the tunes. This made Bill very happy – and Susie, too!

The Sunny Lands

Roger Rabbit had a special gift. He could talk to the birds. Some of the birds used to tell him tales of distant lands where the sun always shone. Roger Rabbit grew very friendly with these birds, but when autumn came and the leaves began to fall, the birds had to say goodbye.

"We're flying off to the distant lands where the sun shines," they chorused. "The winter is *far* too cold for us, so we must go now before it is too late. But we'll see you again next spring. Goodbye Roger!"

Poor Roger was *so* upset. The friendly birds had gone, and they wouldn't be back for such a long time. . .

Roger Rabbit's family and friends tried to cheer him up. But Roger remained a sad rabbit until Carl Caterpillar suggested:

"Why don't you build yourself a little aeroplane? Then you can fly away to see the sunny lands with the birds next autumn."

Roger was so excited about the idea that he began building his aeroplane the very next day.

When the birds returned the following spring, Roger told them about his aeroplane. Summer passed, and they all had a wonderful time together.

When autumn came, Roger was ready to fly off with his feathered friends to the sunny lands. All his family and neighbours came to see him off.

"See you next spring!" they cried, as he took off in his aeroplane and waved goodbye.

Underwater Rabbit

Professor Bobtail was a very clever rabbit. (He knew that the moon is not made of cheese and that carrots don't grow on trees.)

Professor Bobtail knew many things, but he didn't know what lived underneath the waves of the sea. He decided to build his own submarine so that he could sail underwater. The submarine had a big window in it because the professor wanted to see exactly who lived under the waves.

One day Professor Bobtail took his submarine out to sea and dived underneath the waves. He looked out of his window and found, to his surprise, an octopus and a dolphin, and lots of fish who were all staring at *him*.

After all, it wasn't every day they saw a rabbit under the sea!

Big Grey Wolf

Big Grey Wolf was striding down the road with a big stick in his hand. He looked very cross indeed!

Two birds pecking at some crumbs in the road flew away quickly when they saw him coming. "Big Grey Wolf is in a bad mood," said one. "We'd better warn the other animals to keep away from him."

The two birds flew along the road warning rabbits and frogs and mice as they went. "Watch out!" they cried. "Big Grey Wolf is coming. And he's in a bad mood!"

Two red squirrels heard that Big Grey Wolf was coming their way so they both hid. One took cover behind a tree and the other hid behind a big red and white toadstool.

When Big Grey Wolf strode past them they heard him muttering to himself. "I'll show them," he was saying. "I'll show them how to hit that ball!"

"I know where Big Grey Wolf is going," chuckled one of the squirrels. "He's going to play rounders on the village green with the Bear family."

Marcus the Mouse

Marcus the Mouse was sniffing in the grass and whistling to himself.
"Ah! What a perfectly splendid day!" he squeaked. "If I were a composer I'd write a song about such a perfectly splendid day—"

WHOOSH! Marcus the Mouse was nearly squashed flat as a great, big dog went hurtling by.

"Good gracious!" squeaked Marcus. "That must be Bingo the Dog, escaped from his owner again. He's obviously chasing a cat. Now what I can't understand," mused Marcus, "is why human beings don't take mice out for a walk with a lead and a collar. We wouldn't take up as much room. We wouldn't cost as much to feed . . . And what's more," added Marcus the Mouse, "we wouldn't go chasing after cats."

Acorns

It was autumn and Sam Squirrel was out collecting acorns. Every time he found an acorn, he put it in his oak tree larder.

"When winter comes it is going to get very cold," he said to himself. "So I need to store up plenty of food now, while it's still warm."

Sam Squirrel shivered. "There's nothing worse than waking up on a cold winter's morning and having no acorn breakfast to keep you warm. And if it wasn't for acorns, I don't know what little squirrels like me would do!"

The Friendly Frog

Ted was enjoying his summer holiday. One morning he was sitting on a stile, wondering where to eat his picnic, when he saw something move in the long grass.

"It's a frog!" exclaimed Ted, when the creature had hopped nearer. The frog stopped and smiled in a friendly way. "Hello, young man," it croaked. Ted was so surprised to hear the frog speak that he nearly fell off the fence!

Soon Ted and the frog were chatting together like old friends. When lunchtime came, the frog showed Ted a secret froggy place where they shared Ted's picnic. When it was time to go home they agreed to meet again next day . . . and every day after that!

The Two Sisters

There were two little sisters who lived in a White Cottage. They were called Lucy and Lily, and they had a dog called Patch. Lucy had dark brown hair and Lily had hair the colour of golden corn.

Patch loved both the sisters very much. He would take turns to go out with each sister to the park.

When he went with Lucy, he watched her collect a few of the wild flowers there and make them into posies for her mother and grandmother. Sometimes Lucy would plant the seeds of wild flowers, so there would always be plenty of flowers growing wild for everyone to enjoy.

When Patch went out with Lily, she would take some bird seed with her and feed the wild birds. The wild birds loved Lily because she fed them when they were cold and hungry in the winter.

Knowing how kind the two sisters were made Patch very happy, and he would wag his tail a lot. When evening came, Lucy and Lily would give Patch his dinner in his favourite bowl. And that would make him wag his tail even more.

Toby's Favourite Pastime

During the day, Toby the Tortoise liked to nibble the grass in the garden. Sometimes he would sit in the sun near his favourite tree and fall asleep.

At other times, Toby the Tortoise would walk to a hole in the garden fence and see if he could see the tortoise next door.

But perhaps Toby's favourite pastime was to read in bed. And, of course, the story he liked best was *The Tortoise and the Hare*.

The Tramp

Ralph Rabbit was surprised to see tramp rabbit sitting beneath the big warren oak tree. He was dressed in an old overcoat and a crumpled hat and he carried a bent umbrella.

"Why do the other rabbits call you a tramp?" asked Ralph.

"Because I like tramping from place to place," replied the old rabbit. "I've visited nearly every rabbit warren in the country."

"But where is your *home?*" asked Ralph, trying hard to understand.

"I feel at home almost anywhere," said the tramp. "Many warrens have an empty burrow where I can sleep and I can always find some wild parsley to eat. Most days I spend my time sitting in the shade of a tall tree and talking to friendly rabbits – like you!"

Bruno's Dream

When Bruno Bear woke up he realised he had just been dreaming. Bruno's dream was so amazing he felt he had to go and tell his friend, Stan Squirrel, about it straight away.

"Stan," said Bruno, "you'll never believe it. I've just had the most wonderful dream!"

"Tell me all about it," gasped Stan, who had never seen his big friend so excited!

"Well," said Bruno, "I was walking through a huge wood, which was full of enormous trees...and on every tree there grew acorns as big as my front door!"

"That *is* amazing!" squeaked Stan, who was now as excited as Bruno. "An acorn that size would feed my whole family for a year! Could you find your way to the wood, Bruno? Perhaps we could go there tomorrow – with my wheelbarrow!"

Little Lamb

Little Lamb went skipping through the grass. "The grass is so green and the ground is so full of bounce – just like me!" he thought to himself.

As he tripped along, Little Lamb saw a bright green hill. "In a hop and a skip and a jump, I'll be at the top of that hill," he said to himself.

And so, with a hop and a skip and a jump, Little Lamb found himself on top of the hill. There he found some juicy green grass and beautiful flowers. "This looks the perfect place to bring my brothers and sisters," smiled Little Lamb.

Acorn Sums

Bob the Squirrel had made his home inside an oak tree. During the autumn he had collected and stored away plenty of acorns to keep himself alive through the cold winter months.

Bob was a very clever squirrel, for while other squirrels slept during the winter months, Bob was learning sums! To teach himself to count, Bob made himself a little counting frame out of acorns and twigs.

Bob was learning very fast with his acorn abacus. He knew that as soon as he had learnt *all* his lessons he would be able to eat the acorns!

127

The Garden Swing

Every Saturday, Ruth Rabbit would visit her Uncle Jeff...

In her Uncle Jeff's garden was a friendly old tree with some very strong branches. One of these branches hung out over the lawn. Uncle Jeff had fixed two ropes over this branch and tied them to a wooden swing.

When Ruth Rabbit came to see Uncle Jeff she had a lovely surprise when he showed her the swing.

Now every Saturday morning Ruth Rabbit enjoys playing on Uncle Jeff's garden swing.

Shooting Stars

A little while ago in Fairyland there were three pixies who had a magic wooden shoe. Every night they would fix up a mast and sail, and float up to the night sky to try and catch some stars. They had such fun! One night they came really close to catching a star, but as they came up close to the star it shot away across the sky.

Have you ever seen a star shoot across the sky? Maybe the pixie boys are still fishing!

The Clever Juggler

Wayne Rabbit was a smart guy – always very sure that he was smarter than the next guy! One day he saw an advertisement for a juggler to entertain the children at a big party. "That would suit me," he said to his faithful friend, Plodder, the tortoise. "As it happens, I could use some ready money!"

"But you aren't a juggler," said Plodder. "Or are you?"

"Not exactly!" Wayne admitted. "But with a bit of practice I'll be as good as any juggler around."

Wayne applied for the job and was told he had to appear the next Saturday at the children's party. "You had better be good," said the voice at the other end of the telephone. "The children don't put up with rubbish!"

The next day Wayne started practising in earnest. He didn't have any balls or clubs or hoops, but with Plodder's help he got together a strange collection of things and began tossing them in the air.

At first he smashed a plate, the cup landed between his long ears and the apple rolled away. How Plodder laughed! He laughed and laughed and he was still laughing a week later – on the very day of the party!

"The children will murder you!" Plodder chuckled. "You're the worst, the most hopeless juggler I've ever seen in my life…"

"Don't worry," said Wayne calmly. "That is exactly what I'm going as – the worst juggler there ever was! The children will love me – especially when I sing my special song and do a little dance routine…"

Wayne was right. The children laughed and laughed just as Plodder had done. Wayne collected a bonus from the party organiser and later on that night he took his friend Plodder out to a grand supper!

129

Wheelbarrow Express

Katy Kitten, Monty Mouse, Sam Squirrel, Dan Dog and Pinky Pig were waiting at the bus stop. They were all very excited because they were going to see Marvo, the famous magician.

"Everyone who arrives early is given a free bag of popcorn!" squeaked Monty Mouse. "I hope our bus comes soon!"

"Last time Marvo came to town he pulled a rabbit out of a hat," said Katy Kitten.

"Talking of rabbits," barked Dan Dog, "here comes Rodney Rabbit with a wheelbarrow!"

"I'm off to see Marvo the Magician!" cried Rodney. "If any of you would like a lift, please hop on board!"

No sooner had the friends climbed into the wheelbarrow than they were zooming along the road!

"I've never known anyone push a wheelbarrow so fast!" gasped Pinky Pig.

"Didn't I tell you, I won a gold medal in the Wheelbarrow Olympics!" grinned Rodney Rabbit.

Jane's Missing Button

Jane was playing hide and seek with her puppy-dog, Patch. It didn't matter where Jane hid, Patch always found her, and when he did, he barked and wagged his tail excitedly.

Even when Jane hid inside the old barrel at the bottom of the garden Patch still managed to find her. That was because Patch saw the button that had been pulled off Jane's coat when she climbed inside the barrel.

When Jane climbed out of the barrel again, she was very upset at losing her button. Clever Patch, with his barking, showed her where it was. Very soon Jane was all smiles again.

The Silver Ball

It was Christmas time and Skip the Mouse could hear everyone enjoying themselves from his mousehole in the skirting board.

"I do hope they've left a Christmas present for me," he squeaked. "Even if it's only cheese wrapped in tinsel."

In the afternoon when everyone was out, Skip played at the foot of the Christmas tree. There, he found a silver ball which had fallen from the Christmas tree. When Skip looked at his reflection in the silver ball it made him laugh.

"There's a funny-faced mouse in there," he chuckled. "And whenever I laugh, he laughs too! I wonder if he's got any cheese?"

131

Porky's Boot

Porky Pig enjoyed two special things – fishing and eating. Whenever he wanted to really enjoy himself he would take his fishing-rod and a picnic basket down to the river-bank. Here he could forget all about the cares of the world and be a really happy pig.

Sometimes Porky's friend Basil Bear would wander down to the river to see whether he could help Porky with the sandwiches, apples and lemonade in his picnic basket! He also enjoyed fishing.

One day Basil Bear caught a boot on the end of his fishing-line! He was just about to throw it back into the river when Porky – who was having a little snack – said, "Please let me try on that boot." It was a perfect fit and very comfortable!

Now every time Porky takes his rod and picnic basket down to the river-bank he isn't trying to catch fish. Porky Pig would like to catch the other boot!

132

Sun Bird

All the animals who knew Betty Bird loved her. All the flowers and the trees loved her. Even the toadstools loved her.

Every morning as the sun rose Betty Bird would sing her beautiful song. It was so beautiful that the rabbits would run from their tunnels into the open just to hear Betty sing.

Betty loved the sun because it filled her world with light. So she sang. And Betty's song gave her friends much happiness.

A little bear from a nearby wood heard all about Betty's song. Each day he would travel over to hear her sing. "Well," he declared, "Betty's song is sweeter than the sweetest honey."

One morning the rabbits were delighted to see the little bear raise his hat to Betty Bird. He'd brought her a present, too. A box of sunflower seeds.

Captain Bill

Once upon a time there was a family of rabbits who lived on a lonely island. When they wanted to buy some food on the mainland they would row ashore in their small boat. But one day the rabbits' boat sprang a leak....

Luckily Captain Bill Pelican heard about their plight and said he would do their shopping for them.

Captain Bill flew to the mainland where he filled his beak with fresh carrots and lettuces for his rabbit friends.

That night the rabbits had a delicious meal and Captain Bill stayed to supper and told the rabbits exciting stories about the sea.

In a Balloon

"Gosh!" said Mole, climbing into the balloon basket. "This should be a great adventure. Now where did I put my parachute?"

"You won't need a parachute," sighed Rat. "And you won't need those flying goggles either. We're only going up to tree-top height."

"But I might fall out!" cried Mole. "I might fall out and land on my head!"

"You won't fall out," said Rat. "My balloon is very safe."

Suddenly, Mole looked down at the ground. "Help!" he cried. "We must be a long way up. Those animals look as small as ants down there."

"They *are* ants," said Rat. "We haven't even taken off yet!"

134

Short-Sighted Rabbit

One day Professor Rabbit (who wore spectacles) was walking through the wood deep in thought. "One and one make two," he muttered to himself. He was so busy muttering to himself he nearly bumped into a green grass snake.

"Hello!" said the green grass snake. "You're the first rabbit I've ever seen wearing glasses."

Professor Rabbit stopped. "Pardon? Did you say something?"

"You're the first rabbit I've seen wearing glasses," repeated the grass snake.

"And you're the first grass snake I've seen wearing a bow tie," said Professor Rabbit.

"What is a bow tie?" asked the grass snake.

"It's that red bow-shaped object on your neck, of course," said the rabbit.

"It's not a bow tie," said the grass snake. "It's my friend Herbert, the red butterfly. He's just drying his wings."

"I think I need a new pair of glasses!" said Professor Rabbit.

Bongo and Pablo

Bongo the Bear liked to sit in his armchair with a book in his paws. His teacher was called Pablo, and Pablo was a parrot.

Pablo would perch on the back of Bongo's chair. When Bongo the Bear saw a word he didn't know he would point to it. Pablo would then tell him what the word meant.

And when Pablo didn't know what the word was, he would fly off and ask his dad, who was a wise old bird.

Being Together

Kitty the Kitten and Mandy the Mouse were very special friends. When Mandy the Mouse wanted to go shopping to buy herself some cheese and biscuits, Kitty the Kitten would go along with her to the supermarket.

And when Kitty the Kitten wanted to go to the fishmonger's to buy herself some fish, Mandy the Mouse would keep her company. Mandy and Kitty liked to be together *wherever* they went.

On the morning of Kitty's birthday, Mandy turned up with a present. "It's a flower from the fields where we play," said Mandy.

"It's lovely!" exclaimed Kitty. "I'll put it in a vase filled with water."

136

Barney Badger Moves House

It was spring and all the woodland animals were busy spring-cleaning. The rabbits had carried their blankets and curtains out of their warren and down to the river-bank, to wash them. The woodmice family's winter bedsocks were hanging on a bramble bush to dry in the warm wind.

Barney Badger knew he should be spring-cleaning, too. Barney didn't like housework and he remembered last year, when he had worked so hard. Dust had flown everywhere in his underground home as he first polished the furniture and then swept the floor. Once the dust had settled again Barney had been dismayed to see that everything looked as drab as it had been before he began!

As he thought about dusters, mops and polish, Barney had a wonderful idea. He remembered an empty cave, just a little way off, that he had seen on his walk the week before. It was clean and airy...just ready for a badger to live in!

Barney stacked all his furniture and belongings in a gigantic pile and trotted off happily to his new home. He was already planning where he would move to when spring-cleaning time came round again!

137

Bertrand the Potter

Bertrand Bear was a potter. He would get a lump of clay and put it on his potter's wheel. Then he would press a pedal with his foot. This made the wheel holding the lump of clay turn quickly. As it turned, Bertrand Bear would shape the piece of clay into a pot.

Marion Mouse often came to watch Bertrand at work.

Bertrand had made Marion a little pot to keep her cheese in, but most of Bertrand's pots were made for other bears – to keep their honey in!

Good Timing

Oh dear! Millie Mouse had overslept and she would be late to see her friend Monty Mouse. They had arranged to meet by a red toadstool in the corner of a big playing field.

Millie combed her whiskers and put on her favourite hat with the red flower and rushed out of her house. "Oh, if only I could fly!" she squeaked to herself.

As she ran, Millie saw a pink balloon lying in the grass. She stopped for a moment and picked up the string of the balloon. Just then a gust of wind blew Millie and the balloon high in the air and over the field, until she landed next to Monty Mouse and the red toadstool!

"Right on time!" gasped Monty in surprise.

Magic Carpet

Chip and Champ, two chipmunk friends, were on holiday. It was a sunny day and they were stretched out in the garden on a cool leaf, reading their favourite stories.

"This story," said Champ, "is about a carpet..."

"A carpet!" giggled Chip. "Who wants to read about carpets?"

"This is a *magic* carpet," explained Champ. "If you sit on it and wish, it will fly through the air to exciting places!"

"Now that *is* interesting," said Chip, thoughtfully. "You've given me an idea."

"What kind of idea?" asked Champ, sitting up.

"Well, how would you like to fly on a magic carpet?" Chip asked.

"Very much," said Champ, "but I don't think we could."

But Chip whistled to the two crows who lived in a nearby tree. He asked them to hold their sunbed leaf in their beaks – and as the birds flapped their strong wings the two friends found themselves flying through the air on a magic leaf carpet!

Tiger Day

Every year, the jungle animals have a special day they call Tiger Day. On that day the tiger has to pretend he's a donkey!

Thomas the Tiger did not like Tiger Day. "It's the silliest day of the year," he snorted. "This year I think I'll hide under a leafy monkey-tree...no one will think of looking there for me. Donkey indeed!"

When Tiger Day came, Thomas the Tiger hid under the monkey-tree and there he fell asleep. As he slept he had a most peculiar dream. In the dream a little monkey was riding on his back! Two parrots had perched on his curly tail and were singing parrot nursery rhymes very loudly. But worst of all – he, Thomas the Tiger, was singing "Ee-aw, ee-aw"...just like a donkey!

When he awoke, Thomas didn't feel properly like a tiger again until he'd cleaned his teeth, washed his face and chased a monkey into a banana tree.

Jim's Kite

Jim was trying to fly his new kite. But there was hardly a puff of wind to keep it in the air. He had tried running with his new kite but it still wouldn't take off.

Jim was about to carry his kite home when he was joined by his friend John.

"I've got an idea," said John. "I'll bring my three-wheel bike. If you climb onto the back, holding your kite, and I pedal hard, we might make your kite fly."

When John came back with his bike, Jim climbed onto the back with his kite and off they went. John pedalled as hard as he could. Soon they were racing down the road. They passed a wood, and a little girl skipping, and a boy with a hoop, and two little puppies running. John pedalled harder and harder.

"The kite is flying at last!" cried Jim.

"If *we'd* have gone any faster, the bike would have taken off too!" laughed John.

Summer Dreams

When Felicity Fieldmouse awoke one bright July morning, she just *knew* it was going to be a warm sunny day.

After eating a peanut for breakfast Felicity strolled outside into the early morning sunshine. She could feel the warm earth under her tiny feet.

The grass had a lovely fragrance and the breeze was gentle. Felicity walked on, past a mushroom and a toadstool, and finally stopped in her favourite place amongst the flowers.

There was *nothing* Felicity liked better than to lie down on a warm summer's day and listen to the rustle of the daisies and the faint tinkling of the bell flowers.

It was the kind of day Felicity had dreamed about all winter . . . and here it was at last!

Willie the Water-vole

Willie the Water-vole lived in a tiny burrow he had dug into the muddy bank of the river.

Willie loved to sit at the entrance to his little house, with his tail dangling in the cool water, and watch the river gurgling by. When the sun shone on the flowers or big raindrops splashed into the water, Willie was always there to see it happen.

Willie often thought how lucky he was to live in such a beautiful place.

Star Attraction

Sam the Seal and Jumbo the Elephant were performing animals in the same circus. They had always been the best of friends. But they had never worked *together,* until one day Jumbo came to watch Sam the Seal playing in the pool.

"I have an idea!" said Jumbo. "Why don't I stand on the edge of the pool and hold a hoop in my trunk . . .?"

Sam the Seal smiled and clapped his flippers together: "Yes! And I can jump out of the water and through the hoop!"

When the circus master saw them playing together he made Sam and Jumbo's act the star attraction at the circus!

Silly Sports

It was the first day of the holidays and the young animals had decided to hold a sports day. They borrowed sacks, flags, eggs and spoons from the school and a whistle from the policeman.

Freddie Fox said he would be in charge and decide the winners. The trouble was that everyone wanted *their* race to happen first!

"Ready, steady, go!" said Freddie, when the animals were lined up for the first race. But when he waved the flag and blew the whistle everyone started at once! There were animals hopping in sacks, waving eggs and spoons, some jumping over sticks and others pole-vaulting.

Terence Tortoise thought he was winning the fifty-metre dash . . . when Kitty Kitten jumped off his shell and headed straight for the pond! Moses Mole got stuck on a pole and one of the young mice flew on the end of his kite right over the wall into the next field! What a mess!

But, at the end of the afternoon, they all agreed their silly sports had been great fun.

Delivering Letters

Toby Bear was a postman. Every morning, while he was out delivering letters, his pet bird Joey was very lonely and looked forward to Toby's return. Toby's rounds took all morning because everyone was pleased to see him and wanted to say hello.

One morning, as Toby was getting ready to leave home, Joey chirped, "May I come with you, Toby?"

"That's a good idea," said Toby. "I could do with some help."

Joey was a clever little bird and soon he was picking up letters in his beak and posting them through people's letter-boxes.

"You should ask the post office for a proper job!" joked Toby.

"Yes!" chirped Joey. "I could see to all the *air*-mail letters."

Susie the Moth

A little moth called Susie was flying towards a tiny light in the sky.

"Oh, I'm so tired," said Susie, "so very tired."

As the light grew brighter and brighter, the little moth finally fell asleep on the wing.

When Susie awoke the next day she found herself on a friendly green leaf.

"I must have dreamt about my tiring journey last night," she sighed to herself. Then she noticed that the end of her wings were sparkling with *stardust*! "Gosh!" whispered Susie. "Perhaps it wasn't a dream after all!"

(Now, if *you* ever see a moth whose wings sparkle with stardust, say "Hello" to Susie!)

The Happy Duck

Farmyard Duck was happy.
"Quack!" She was looking forward to a quick paddle in her favourite pond in Duckland. So off she went through the farmyard gates, leaving the cows to moo and the king of the hens to cock-a-doodle-doo.

Farmyard Duck went waddling through the grass where daisies grew like stars. Past a big oak tree with spring-time leaves.

"Quack!" Farmyard Duck could smell her favourite pond ahead. Only another short waddle and *splash*! into the pond!

What would make her day complete, she thought as she paddled around, would be if someone brought bread to feed her.

"Two slices please, but no cream quackers!"

Heatwave

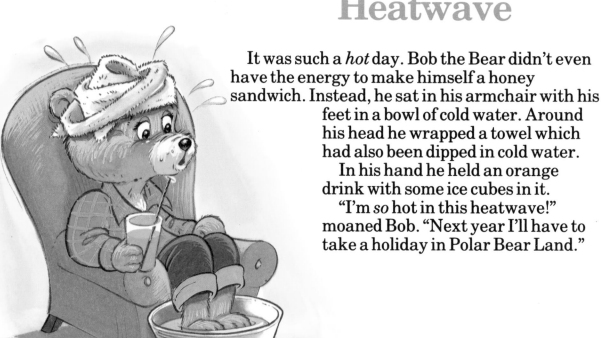

It was such a *hot* day. Bob the Bear didn't even have the energy to make himself a honey sandwich. Instead, he sat in his armchair with his feet in a bowl of cold water. Around his head he wrapped a towel which had also been dipped in cold water.

In his hand he held an orange drink with some ice cubes in it.

"I'm *so* hot in this heatwave!" moaned Bob. "Next year I'll have to take a holiday in Polar Bear Land."

146

Rainbow Butterfly

Bella the Butterfly had beautiful wings. Every colour of the rainbow seemed to glow from Bella's wings as she flew. The birds and animals who lived nearby called Bella the Rainbow Butterfly. Bella liked the name Rainbow Butterfly, but she had never seen a *real* rainbow.

However, one day Bella was fluttering between the trees during a shower when suddenly the sun came out. There, in the sky ahead, a great coloured arch appeared, stretching right across the sky.

"Oh, that is lovely!" gasped Bella, settling on a shiny leaf. "I wonder what it can be."

147

Sailor Mouse

Freddie Fieldmouse was out for his morning run. "This is the kind of day that makes you feel bouncy and happy!" squeaked Freddie, as he jogged along. He was going so fast that he bumped into an empty yoghurt pot!

"This empty pot will make a wonderful boat!" said Freddie, when he had stopped panting. "And here is a spoon I can use as an oar. I can row down stream to visit my old friend Willie Water-vole."

So Freddie put on his smart sailor hat and set off in his new boat. All the animals smiled and waved as he paddled past. He had so much fun in his new boat that he now visits Willie Water-vole every day!

Sam's Snorkel

While he was at the seaside, Sam borrowed his dad's diving goggles and snorkel.

"I want to swim in the rock pool," said Sam to his dad. "Will you come and watch me?"

"Okay," agreed his dad. "You can pretend you're a submarine."

When Sam swam underwater for the first time, everything looked so different! He could hardly believe his eyes when a fish swam towards him.

"Dad's snorkel helps me to breathe underwater," thought Sam, "but I wonder how all the sea animals manage to breathe underwater *without* a snorkel?"

148

Balloons

It was an autumn day and the leaves were turning brown on the trees. In the park the children were playing. A gentle wind was blowing across the grass and songbirds were singing.

Sarah looked up into the sky and saw a golden ball drifting through the air. "Look!" she gasped. "What is it? It's almost the colour of sunshine!"

The other children stopped playing and watched as the golden ball slowly floated higher and higher.

"It's a balloon," said one of the boys.

"Yes. But where did it come from?" asked his friend.

Then Sarah saw a man in a blue cap standing under a tree at the edge of the park. "Look!" she cried, pointing. "There's a man selling balloons."

As the children ran towards him, the man called: "Balloons! Big ones, small ones. Choose your own colours."

"I'd like a purple one, please," said Sarah.

Tom's New Tricycle

Tom the Terrier had bought a new tricycle. The first thing he did was to go and see his friend Carla the Cat.

"How do you like my new tricycle?" asked Tom the Terrier.

"I think it's really cute," purred Carla the Cat. "How do you like my new stripy dungarees?"

"I think they're cute, too," said Tom. "How would you like a ride on my new tricycle?"

"I'd like that very much," purred Carla the Cat. "Can we go into the country and hear the birds sing?"

So they went into the country, and the very first bird they saw made them both very happy by flying along with them and singing a lovely song.

Sleepy Time

Matilda Mouse was sitting on top of her favourite stone. The sun had been shining earlier in the day, and now the stone was nice and warm. It was pleasant sitting there in the warmth and the gentle breeze.

"All in all," thought Matilda Mouse, "it's the perfect afternoon for a snooze."

Matilda was just closing her eyes to have a mouse-nap, when she felt a tickle on top of her head.

"Oh," she said. "What is that tickle on the top of my head?"

"I'm not a tickle," said a little voice. "I'm a butterfly. And I was just thinking of going to sleep. You see, it's so nice and warm here on top of your head. And I'm – gosh – so tired."

150

Crossing the River

Mrs Millie Rabbit had lived near the banks of the River Flow for a great many years. She liked it there because she had a nice cosy home and was very friendly with the water rats who lived next door.

But although Mrs Millie Rabbit was very happy, she did *so* want to visit her brother Mr Montgomery Rabbit who lived on the other side of the river.

The problem was: how could she cross the river? There were no bridges and the River Flow was such a quiet river that no boats ever passed that way.

One day, Spot the Dog heard about Mrs Rabbit's problem and said he would help. With logs and planks of wood, Spot built a raft, and rowed Mrs Rabbit across to see her brother.

Mrs Millie Rabbit was delighted. And so was her brother Montgomery who hadn't seen her for such a long time.

Rabbits Can't Fly!

Tilly the Rabbit was bobbing along when she heard Bluebird singing.

"It's a beautiful morning and singing makes me happy," chirped the little bird.

Tilly the Rabbit hopped along a bit further until she came to the little pool where Green Frog lived.

"Hello, Green Frog," greeted Tilly. "You look happy!"

"I am happy," said Green Frog. "I've been sitting croaking on my favourite stone all morning."

Tilly walked on a little way. "I wonder what it's like to fly like Bluebird?" mused Tilly. "And I wonder what it's like to swim like Green Frog?"

So Tilly decided – just this once – to try and fly like Bluebird. She went home and picked up her umbrella. Then she climbed a tree near Green Frog's pool and with the umbrella open like a parachute, Tilly jumped off a branch.

"But rabbits can't fly!" squawked Bluebird.

"You're right!" groaned Tilly as she fell –

splash – into the pond. "And they can't swim very well either," croaked Green Frog.

"In future I'll stick to being a rabbit," spluttered Tilly the Rabbit. "After all it's what makes *me* happy!"

The Friendly Spider

Tommy and Tilly Fieldmouse had been given some badminton rackets by their Great Aunt Matilda. So, as it was a sunny May morning they went out into the fields to play.

They started by hitting the shuttlecock backwards and forwards to each other, but they soon got bored with this.

"What we need is a net," said Tilly. "Then we can have a *proper* game."

"Hello!" said Simon Spider, dangling down on a thread from the branch of an oak tree. "Would you like me to spin you a net?"

"Yes, please! If it wouldn't be too much trouble," said Tommy.

"No trouble," said Simon Spider. "I often spin nets so fieldmice can play games of badminton." And in five minutes Simon Spider had done just that!

"Would you like me to stay and watch you play?" asked Simon after he'd finished.

"Yes, do!" said Tilly. "And you can be umpire and keep the score if you like."

Moonlight Millie

Millie Mouse liked to sleep out of doors. She loved to watch the moon shining in the night sky. She also liked to see the friendly stars twinkling.

One day, when Millie Mouse was out walking, she found an empty box. Millie filled the box with dried grass and herbs and put the box under her favourite daisy.

"This will make a lovely bed," said Millie Mouse. "Tonight I'll sleep here under the stars with my favourite daisy to watch over me."

Safely Home

Captain Morgan kept his boat in the harbour near the lighthouse. One morning he was up very early, packing sandwiches and fresh orange juice for a trip across Windy Bay to see his uncle.

Captain Morgan never liked crossing Windy Bay. The strong currents always made his boat difficult to steer and the wind made the waves roll and splash against her sides. It was a bright morning when Captain Morgan set out and the crossing was easy.

He spent a pleasant day with his uncle, talking about sailing ships and sea-fishing.

On the way back, the sea was rough. Captain Morgan kept calm.

He peered into the darkness towards the harbour . . . and, sure enough, there was the lighthouse light, winking to guide him home. Soon he was safely in the harbour, thanks to the lighthouse.

Mrs McMouse's Tea Party

Mrs McMouse made the best cup of tea in Green Leaf Woods. Friends would call from near and far just to taste Mrs McMouse's tea. She also made very tasty cakes and pastries.

Mrs McMouse lived in Melon Cottage, not far from Deep Down Well. It was one of the nicest parts of Green Leaf Wood.

One day a stranger came to live on High Top Hill, overlooking Green Leaf Woods. His name was Sir Basil B. Badger.

"He sounds very important, I'm sure," said Mrs McMouse. "And we'll have to make him feel welcome in his new home."

So Mrs McMouse and her friends laid on a teatime treat especially for Sir Basil B. Badger. When Sir Basil B. Badger tasted Mrs McMouse's tea, he said, "Mrs McMouse, you make the best tea I've *ever* tasted, and your cakes are delicious too!"

That made everyone feel very happy, and very pleased for Mrs McMouse.

Leap-Frog

Wendy and John and their dog, Pip, were playing with a hoop. As the hoop rolled through the park, Wendy, John and Pip chased after it. They ran down a path which led through the trees.

After a while they came to a little playground where four boys were playing leap-frog. Wendy and John stopped their hoop and watched the boys enjoying themselves. Pip the dog watched too with his head on one side.

One boy would bend forward and the other three would leap over him like frogs. Then another boy would bend forward and the others would take their turn at leap-frog.

Suddenly Pip the dog ran up to the boys.

"Look!" said Wendy. "Pip wants to play leap-frog too!"

"But he won't be able to leap *that* high!" gasped John.

"Gruff!" barked Pip as he ran forward. And then he leap-frogged – right over a clump of daisies!

156

Pixie Pete's Rescue

Pixie Pete lived in an old kettle by the river. Like all pixies, Pete had long pointed ears which helped him to hear all kinds of things. Pixie Pete could hear the flowers talk to each other, and when the wind blew Pete would hear the trees whispering.

One day, when Pete was making himself a cup of pixie tea in his kettle home, he heard a sound he didn't like! He rushed outside and saw that a litle pixie had fallen into the river.

"Help!" cried the little pixie. "Help! I can't swim!"

"Oh dear!" gasped Pete. "What should I do?"

"Use me as a boat," whispered a nearby flower. "And rescue the little pixie."

"What a good idea!" cried Pixie Pete. And in the twinkling of a pixie's eye, Pete had turned up the flower and was sailing towards the little pixie.

As Pete pulled the little pixie aboard the flower boat, he said, "Come back and have a cup of tea in my kettle home. Then I'll teach you how to swim!"

Cyril the Squirrel

Every winter Cyril the Squirrel would go to sleep in his tree home. When cold winds blew Cyril would be wrapped up cosily in his blanket of leaves and grass.

Cyril had never seen the snow . . . because while the ponds were frozen and the children were making snowmen, Cyril would be fast asleep and dreaming of springtime.

It was only when the weather turned warmer, when the leaves came back to the trees and the spring flowers blossomed, that Cyril would at last wake up. Then he would stand in his doorway, stretch himself and yawn – and thank heaven for springtime! Would you like to be a squirrel?

Sailing in the Sun

Teddy Toad and George Grasshopper were very good friends. But Teddy Toad liked *wet* weather, and George Grasshopper liked *dry* weather.

Naturally George Grasshopper didn't enjoy visiting Teddy Toad's home by the river-bank because it was so damp. So Teddy Toad suggested they go boating in a big water-lily leaf.

With the sun shining brightly, George Grasshopper was able to keep nice and dry in the water-lily boat. And to keep himself happy, Teddy Toad kept diving overboard into the water for a swim.

Mrs Green's Garden

Mrs Green lived in a cottage on top of a grassy bank. Behind the cottage were lots of trees, and at the foot of the grassy bank was a garden. There were lots of flowers in Mrs Green's garden.

In the winter Mrs Green would feed the birds and squirrels and the rabbits because she knew that they needed plenty to eat in the cold weather.

One day Mrs Green took a train to see her sister who lived in the city. She was going to stay with her sister for a month, and when she returned to her cottage she expected to find her garden full of weeds.

But the squirrels and rabbits liked Mrs Green so much that when she was away they did some gardening for her. They dug out the weeds and watered the flowers and made sure everything stayed neat and tidy.

When Mrs Green came home, the grass on the bank had been nibbled short by the rabbits, and her garden was bright with flowers.

Tim and the Owl

One day Tim borrowed a book about birds from the library. It had wonderful coloured pictures and Tim read it in bed every night. There were eagles, wrens, penguins and owls.

One night, just as Tim was closing his eyes to go to sleep, he heard a noise by the window. Tim saw two big, round eyes blinking through the darkness. He remembered the pictures in his book – and he knew that owls were busy at night. Yes! It *was* an owl!

Tim was pleased that he had recognised the bird and the next morning he told his mother what had happened.

"I wonder if owls read in bed, too?" she said.

Sad Suzy

Suzy was feeling so sad. She woke up feeling sad, and even after breakfast she *still* felt sad.

So Suzy combed her fur and tied her best ribbon on her head and went out into the fresh air. As soon as she saw the pretty flowers she felt just a *little* better.

"I'm not as sad as I was before," she said to herself. "But I'm still not really happy."

Just then two tiny bluebirds passed by. They saw Suzy looking glum, so they flew down beside her.

"We'll cheer you up," chirped one of the bluebirds. "We'll sing a duet for you."

"Yes, please. I'd like that," said Suzy. "And I'm sure that *will* cheer me up!"

160

Treasure Chest

It was a dull, rainy day and Mummy had promised James and Jennie that they could play in the attic.

"You might find some things up there for your school play," said Mummy.

When the children began to explore the attic they found some *very* interesting things. Jennie found some of the toys Mummy had played with when she was a girl. James discovered an old football book which belonged to Daddy. Suddenly James whispered, "Look, Jennie! I've found a treasure chest!"

When the children looked inside the chest they found some old fashioned clothes. "These are just what we need for the school play!" said Jennie. "Let's dress up in them now and give Mummy a surprise when we go down for tea!"

Monkey Business

There was thunder and lightning over Monkey Village. Rain poured down, splashing off the leaves. Small puddles grew into large puddles. Large puddles turned into lakes. The sky grew darker, and the rain still poured down.

"This looks bad," shouted the Chief of the Monkeys, choking on his banana. "We must do something."

"We could re-build Monkey Village on stilts," suggested Wise Monkey.

"It's a bit late for that," said the Monkey Chief. "Anyone got any better ideas?"

"Let's build a boat," piped up Tiny Monkey. "Then we can float around until the waters go down."

"That's a good idea," admitted the Wise Monkey.

"But what kind of boat?" asked the Chief. "What shape should it be?"

"Why not a banana-shaped boat?" said Tiny Monkey.

"A splendid idea, Tiny Monkey!" beamed Chief Monkey. "One day you might become Chief Monkey."

"He'll need to eat a lot more bananas before he's big enough," muttered the jealous Wise Monkey.

162

The Homesick Frog

"I'm tired of swimming around the same old pond," complained Green Frog. "What I need is a big lake. Somewhere I can stretch my legs and croak all day long in the bulrushes."

"I know where there's a big lake," said Colin Cat. "It's near the big hill."

"But it's much too far for a little frog like me to travel!" croaked Green Frog. "I'd get blisters on my green feet."

"I could carry you there," suggested Colin Cat.

"Yes, but how?" asked Green Frog.

"Well, I simply fill a bucket with water," said Colin. "And I carry you to the lake in the bucket."

"I like it. I like it," croaked Green Frog. "Big lake – here I come!"

Ralph Rabbit

Ralph Rabbit had a home-made wheelbarrow. He had made it himself, fixing two wheels and two handles to an old wooden box.

Ralph liked to wander along country paths pushing his wheelbarrow. Sometimes he would walk for miles.

Ralph had a friend called Dora the Duck. Dora was a big white farmyard duck and she didn't like walking *too* far.

So when Dora saw Ralph out walking she would hitch a ride in his wheelbarrow!

163

Magic Crumbs

One fine day a little mouse was tip-toeing through the grass in search of crumbs. After a short time he found five crumbs hidden under a toadstool. So the mouse picked up a nice round crumb, sat down on the toadstool and began to eat the crumb.

"This should keep me squeaking for a while," squeaked the mouse to himself.

"Hello," said a voice.

"Squeak!" said the mouse, nearly dropping his crumb.

"Don't be frightened," said the voice. (It was such a nice, musical voice.)

When the mouse looked up, he saw a beautiful daisy smiling down at him.

"Oh, hello," said the mouse. "I didn't know flowers could talk."

"Of course we can talk," laughed the daisy. "But very few people or animals can hear us. But you've been eating magic crumbs which help you to hear us."

"Can I come tomorrow and eat some more magic crumbs?" asked the mouse. "You've got such a nice voice and I'd like to hear you sing."

"Of course," smiled the daisy. "Please do."

164

Good Morning

A little fallow deer called Merry lived in the woods. It was early morning and the sun beamed down. Little flowers glowed blue, yellow and purple in the grass.

Merry was standing under a big beech tree nibbling at a leaf when a butterfly fluttered by.

"Good morning," said Merry.

"Good morning," replied the butterfly. "What a *lovely* morning!"

"Yes. It makes me feel like skip-skipping through the grass," said Merry.

"And it makes me feel like flutter-fluttering through the air," said the butterfly.

So off they went, with the butterfly fluttering and Merry skip-skipping. And the sun beamed down, and the little flowers glowed.

What a lovely morning it was!

Sam Bear

Sam Bear was a hat maker and he had made top hats for many famous bears. Sam Bear had also been saving empty honey barrels. . . .

One morning, Sam Bear woke up with a bright idea in his head. He would use some of his honey barrels and try and make top hats out of them. Sam made the first honey barrel hat for himself.

Now all the bears in Sam's town are wearing honey barrel hats.

166

Pedro the Pirate

Pedro the pirate was very excited; he had just heard about some treasure on the seabed a little way off the Isle of Coconuts. He chuckled as he got ready his old pirate ship.

"The sea around the island is very clear; all I'll have to do is sail slowly round, peering into the water," he said. "It won't take long to find that treasure... then I'll be a rich man! I'll call myself Baron Pedro and buy a castle and have lots of servants. I shall never have to work again... I'll be on holiday for the rest of my life!"

Pedro the pirate found the treasure chest, just as he thought he would – but Oswald Octopus had got there first!

Pedro threw out the ship's anchor and leaned over the side. "Right!" he shouted to Oswald. "Hand over the treasure!"

"Oh no!" gurgled the octopus. "I'm guarding this treasure for Captain Blowhorn, the famous pirate hunter – who should be here any minute!"

Parcel Post

Emma Jane had lost her kitten. The kitten, whose name was Fluffy, had gone into the garden, climbed over the fence and disappeared. Poor Emma Jane was very upset. She looked all that day, but couldn't find Fluffy.

Three days later Emma Jane received a parcel; a box with holes in the lid – and something moving inside! When Emma Jane opened it she found Fluffy! There was a note explaining that the kitten had climbed into a furniture van and fallen asleep. The driver had driven many miles before he heard Fluffy calling! Luckily, Fluffy's collar had her address on it; the van driver had seen this and sent the kitten home – by parcel post.

The Yellow Spectacles

Arnold the Alligator was swimming along in the river – when suddenly
he felt like having a chat with a friend. "I'll go and talk to my friend
Archie," he said to himself.

After Arnold the Alligator had paddled a few metres, he saw a shape
which looked like Archie the Alligator floating in the water ahead.

"Hello, Archie," said Arnold. "Miserable weather we're having."

Archie didn't say anything.

"He must be asleep," said Arnold. "I'll have to speak up. Hello, Archie!"
he cried.

Archie still didn't say anything.

Then Arnold realised he'd mistaken a floating tree trunk for his friend
Archie. "I'll have to go and get myself some spectacles," muttered Arnold.
"Green ones? No. I'd probably lose them in the grass. I know, I'll get myself
a pair of *yellow* spectacles."

168

The Rabbit and the Butterfly

Roger the Rabbit was snoozing on a mound of earth. Flowers grew nearby, giving off delicious scents. It was nice and warm. Roger could feel his nose twitching and it made him open one eye.

"Ooh! Oh! What's that?" he cried, blinking. A butterfly had landed right on the end of Roger's nose!

"Hello, Flutterby," said Roger.

"Hello, Rabbit," said the butterfly. "But why do you call me a flutterby?"

"Sorry, Butterfly," said Roger the Rabbit. "I didn't mean to be rude. But I often see you fluttering by. And you don't *look* like a fly. And I've never seen you eat butter. So that's why I called you a flutterby."

Three Little Chicks

Harriet Hen was the proudest hen in the farmyard. She was the mother of three lovely little chicks.

"When my three little chickens grow up," she said, "they'll be top of the class at chicken school. And when they grow up to be hens, they'll be good hens, just like their mum!"

Even before they went to school, the three little chicks knew that *one and one makes two* and *one and two makes three* and *not to go with any strange foxes.*

"I want my three little chickens to be fit and strong little chickens," said Harriet Hen.

So every morning at sunrise, Harriet Hen took them out jogging!

169

Major Mole's Big Band

Major Mole was very proud of his band. Every Friday evening the players met in the village hall. They wore their smart red uniforms and practised hard on their shiny instruments for two hours. They really sounded very good indeed.

One Friday Major Mole announced that the mayor was arriving at the village station the next day. "We have been asked to march along the platform and play our music," he told the players. What an honour!

Next morning the band lined up, looking smarter than ever. "One, two, three, four..." shouted Major Mole.

"Left, right, left, right..." said the musicians, stepping off after him. Oh dear! The band had never tried to play *and* march before – and everything went wrong!

However, Major Mole did have a letter from the mayor, saying how much he had enjoyed their music – but he didn't mention their marching!

The Tired Train

It was a lovely hot summer's day and the little old yellow railway train puff-puffed up the steep hill.

"Gosh – puff – this is hard work!" puffed the little old yellow train.

Normally the little train would chuff-chuff-chuff up the hill, tooting its whistle, wheels going clickity-clack at top speed. But this day was so terribly hot, the carriages were heavy and the hill seemed so steep.

"I – puff – must rest," gasped the little yellow train. "I'm so – puff – worn out. But I'll be all right in a – puff – minute."

The little train slowed to a halt and stopped on the hill. It was completely out of puff and soon fell asleep.

"Well, well. Tut, tut. What's wrong?" muttered the guard, stroking his beard and checking his watch.

All the people and animals on board poked their heads out of the windows of the carriages. "What's wrong?" they echoed.

But the engine driver knew the old train had fallen asleep. He could see the ZZzz shaped steam coming out of the engine.

"The old train is snoring!" he chuckled.

Screecher the Monkey

Screecher the Monkey wanted to sing nearly all the time. The trouble was – Screecher the Monkey couldn't sing very well. In fact, his singing was so bad that the jungle animals would hide or cover their ears if they saw Screecher coming.

One wise old elephant even stuck coconuts in his ears so he couldn't hear a note that Screecher sang.

Screecher had two pals called Monty and Maurice and they would all play in the jungle together, swinging in the trees and eating bananas. If Screecher wanted to start singing when he was with Monty and Maurice, they'd tell him to climb into a tree and sing by himself.

When Screecher was singing high in a tree, Monty and Maurice couldn't hear him. And usually Screecher's awful voice would make some of the leaves and bananas fall off the trees. With the leaves Monty and Maurice would make a nice warm bed for themselves. And, of course, they'd eat the bananas!

Joe the Clown

Joe was a housepainter. In his wheelbarrow he carried pots of paint and brushes. Across the top of his barrow he carried his stepladders.

Sometimes he would fall off his ladder and land on his head and other times he would put his foot in a pot of paint.

Joe began to think about that. He thought: "If I put my foot in a pot of paint, people think I'm a bad housepainter. But if I were a clown, they'd think I was a *good* clown."

So Joe became a clown. And a very good clown too!

Tweet and Twitter

Tweet and Twitter were two very friendly little birds, and everybody liked seeing them around.

But one year the winter was harsher than it had ever been before and people were so busy keeping warm and well-fed that they forgot all about their little friends, Tweet and Twitter.

"You would think somebody would invite us to share their warm kitchen," said Tweet. "We only have this branch for a perch and I'm so cold I don't know how long I can perch on it..."

"It's the same with me," said Twitter. "I thought we had so many good friends – now I don't think we have any..."

But he was wrong! Not far away, little Miss Lavender was busy knitting. She used all her odd bits of wool and made little woolly caps and thick, warm mufflers. Then she went to her front door and called the two birds down from their perch. Soon they were enjoying warm bread and milk and when it was time to go, they were warmly dressed in woolly caps and mufflers!

173

The Big Joke

Cuthbert Clown was very unhappy because the Circus Master was always playing tricks on him. Sometimes the Circus Master would hide Cuthbert Clown's false nose, or put a clockwork mouse in his hat. One day the Circus Master even put liquorice shoe-laces in Cuthbert's long, flat circus shoes. This upset Cuthbert so much he decided to go and talk to the Circus Master.

When he heard Cuthbert complaining, the Circus Master laughed. "But you're a clown!" he cried. "You should be able to laugh at my little jokes!"

"How would you like me to play a joke on *you*?" asked Cuthbert.

"It wouldn't worry me at all," declared the Circus Master.

The next day the Circus Master received a large box. When he opened it he was so surprised he fell over with a bump! Out from the box had jumped a huge puppet policeman on a spring!

"This must be from Cuthbert," gasped the Circus Master when he had recovered from the shock. "Now I understand that tricks aren't always funny!"

Crossing the Road

Grandma Cat was nearly ninety years old! She had lived in Tabby Town all her life. There had been no motorcars in Tabby Town when Grandma was a kitten; instead, horses pulled carriages through the quiet streets.

Now that Grandma Cat was nearly ninety years old everything had changed. The streets of Tabby Town were very busy and noisy. Just watching the cars and motorcycles roaring up and down the road made Grandma Cat feel dizzy!

When Billy Cat came to stay with Grandma he showed her a safe place to cross the road.

"This is a special cat crossing," explained Billy. "You stand on the pavement and wait until the light tells you it is safe to cross."

"Isn't it wonderful," purred Grandma Cat as the lights changed. "All the traffic is stopping so we can cross the road safely. I'll always use the special crossing in future!"

Friendly Tortoise

Tony Tortoise got up bright and early to go mushroom picking. After washing his wrinkly face and drinking a mug of lettuce tea, Tony set out for the mushroom fields.

"I must make sure I don't pick any toadstools by mistake," said Tony to himself. He remembered his mother telling him never to eat toadstools.

When Tony reached the fields he found lots of pretty flowers and lots of toadstools... but no mushrooms!

Tony felt very tired after his long walk. "Oh dear," he yawned. "I think I'd better have a snooze by a tall, shady tree before I go home."

Much later, Tony was woken by his two friends Sam and Scamp Squirrel.

"We've been trying to find you all morning!" gasped Scamp.

"Why? Whatever is the matter?" asked Tony, sleepily.

"Nothing is the matter," explained Sam. "We have collected all these mushrooms for you, because you're such a nice, friendly tortoise!"

The Music Man

Bobby's uncle was a musician. He could play so many instruments that he decided to become a one-man-band.

This is how he did it. In his hands he held a concertina. Between his legs were fixed some cymbals. On his back was a big bass drum. In his pocket was a flute. And a metal support around his neck made sure his trumpet was always there, ready to blow into.

He gave Bobby a demonstration one day and made such a noise the neighbours thought it was a brass band.

"I'd like to be a music man when I grow up," smiled Bobby.

"You can start by whistling along to this next tune," said his uncle.

The Top Hat

The day after the circus left town Francis Frog went out for a hop. He hadn't gone very far before he found an old top hat upside down in the grass. Overnight it had filled with clear rainwater.

"I've found a great big top hat," Francis told his friend Marty Mouse, "and it's the perfect place for us to swim!"

"A top hat!" squeaked Marty. "How can anyone swim in a top hat?"

"Just you come and see!" croaked Francis, who was very excited about his discovery.

Half an hour later the two friends croaked and squeaked with delight as they dived from the hat's brim and swam and splashed in the cool, fresh water.

Flipper Frog

Flipper Frog was very big and very green; he had strong froggy legs and liked to hop from place to place. Over his shoulder he always carried a stick and tied to the end of the stick was a handkerchief full of magic tricks.

Flipper Frog hopped along at an amazing speed. The only time he stopped was when he was hungry, or thirsty, or sleepy – or when one of the animals wanted to see a magic trick.

One day Flipper Frog was hopping along the lane when Polly and Perky Squirrel asked if he would show them one of his magic tricks.

"What kind of trick would you like to see?" asked Flipper.

"Please show us the one where you make chestnuts appear from nowhere!" requested Polly.

"Very well," said Flipper, opening his handkerchief and hopping up and down excitedly. Just at that moment two large chestnuts fell out of the tree above them!

"Well, now," croaked Flipper with delight. "It seems you don't need frog magic to make chestnuts appear!"

The Friendly Snowman

One winter's day Barney Bear built a snowman in his garden. Barney Bear wrapped an old scarf around the snowman's neck and put an old hat on the snowman's head. During the long winter, Barney and the snowman became good friends.

"I'd like to be your friend for ever," said Barney Bear.

"I'd like that too," answered the friendly snowman. "But when the warmer weather comes, I'll have to go. You see, I need to stay cold all the time."

Suddenly Barney smiled. He had just remembered that it was *always* cold at the local ice-rink.

Now the snowman lives happily at the ice-rink in the town during the warm weather and has lots of new friends who see him when they go there to skate. But when the really cold weather comes again, the friendly snowman is a welcome visitor to the garden outside Barney Bear's home.

179

Darren Dog

Darren Dog was tired of living in a dog kennel. "What I'd really like," he told his friend Bertie Bird, "is to fly, like you."

"But you'd need a pair of wings for that," replied Bertie.

"Yes, I know," sighed Darren.

"So why don't you build an aeroplane?" suggested Bertie.

"What a good idea! I'll begin right away. I've already got four wheels and a horn to start with."

Darren Dog spent seven long months building his aeroplane; it was very hard work, but great fun, too. When it was finished, however, Darren wasn't sure his aeroplane *could* fly.

"Tuck a parachute into your hat – just in case," said Bertie Bird. "I'll be close behind you. Good luck!"

"Thanks, Bertie," said Darren, nervously.

Five minutes later Darren Dog was flying high in the sky – with a parachute hidden under his hat, just in case!

The Tree Seat

One day Lucy Rabbit went to see her friend Randolph, who was a painter.

"I'd like you to paint a picture for me, please," said Lucy.

"Certainly," replied Randolph Rabbit. "What is it you'd like me to paint for you?"

"Well," said Lucy. "Deep in Happy Tree Wood there is a tree trunk where I love to sit; I'd like you to paint my favourite tree trunk for me, please."

"Come along then," said Randolph, gathering his paints and brushes. "Show me where this special tree trunk is."

After quite a long walk the two rabbits were deep inside the wood. Lucy showed Randolph the tree trunk and he thought for a moment. "I think it would be a good idea if you sat on your tree seat – then I will paint a picture of you both!"

Now that painting of Lucy and her favourite tree seat hangs over the fireplace in her burrow. On cold winter days, when Lucy cannot go out to the wood, the picture reminds her of warm and happy times.

Express Tortoise

Tim Tortoise knew he had to walk down another steep, snowy hill before he could reach his home. To make matters worse, his little tortoise toes were freezing!

As Tim Tortoise plodded down the hill he closed his eyes...

"I wish I could be outside my house at the bottom of this long hill," he whispered to himself.

At that moment Tim tripped and rolled onto his back. His smooth, hard shell acted like a super toboggan – and he went sliding down the hill faster than a rabbit can run!

Soon Tim was back indoors, happily eating a lettuce sandwich and warming his tiny toes in front of a warm, cosy fire.

The Butterfly

Simon was playing in his grandfather's garden when something bright and colourful flew over his head.

He turned round quickly and saw a butterfly fluttering over the large daisies near the sundial. Simon stayed very still until the creature settled on an open flower. He tiptoed towards it.

The butterfly had large wings of beautiful colours, each with a matching pattern. Simon had never seen anything like it before.

"Try not to disturb it, Simon," said his grandfather in a whisper.

"I won't," said Simon, holding his breath. "I'll watch until it flies away and then draw a picture of the butterfly and paint its lovely colours – if I can remember them."

Fred Tuttle

Fred Tuttle was a very clever man. He was an expert on everything from crocodiles to hamsters.

Fred had written a great many books. His first book had been about rabbits. Fred's second book was all about carrots and his third book explained why carrots are most rabbits' favourite food.

When Fred Tuttle started to write a book about dogs his pet dog Scamp was so pleased he couldn't stop wagging his tail! Every time Fred wrote a line for the book he would read it out loud to see what Scamp thought of it.

"The dog is a very clever animal," read Fred.

"Woof! Woof!" barked Scamp in agreement.

"A dog is often called a man's best friend," read Fred.

"Woof! Woof! Woof!" barked Scamp again.

"Dogs always enjoy being taken for a walk," read Fred.

"Woof! Woof! Woof! Woof!" barked Scamp, rushing round the untidy room and wagging his tail.

"And I'm going to take Scamp, *my* dog, for a walk right now!" chuckled Fred.

The Three Friends

There was only one thing Rinty Rhino liked better than bathing in a big pool of squelchy mud... that was to see his two special friends. One of Rinty's friends was called Bluebird; the other friend's name was Boris Bunny.

When Rinty had a day off from the zoo he liked to meet Bluebird and Boris in a shady field at the edge of a wood. Here they would talk and sing and laugh and tell each other stories.

Rinty Rhino told marvellous tales of the big lakes and rivers in Africa. Boris Bunny told his friends about life down under the earth in a cosy rabbit warren. Bluebird sang songs about the wind, the sky and the treetops.

Being good friends, Boris and Bluebird didn't forget Rinty's birthday. Boris Bunny brought Rinty a ripe banana – his favourite fruit – and Bluebird made him a garland of fresh flowers for his pointed horn.

184

Terry Tiger

Terry Tiger lived in a smart wooden house at the edge of Marigold Meadow. He was known by all the other animals to be a very clever tiger and liked nothing better than to sit down under a tree and read a book. His favourite was *The Wonder Book of Nature*, which had been written a long time before by Terry's grandfather, Horatio Tiger.

The animals of Marigold Meadow often saw Terry out walking, looking for a shady tree. Sometimes they would ask him questions about nature. They weren't surprised to find that Terry had an answer for everything!

One day, Roger Rabbit and Stewart Kitten asked Terry a *very* difficult question.

"Terry," they giggled, "can you please tell us why bees make such a funny buzzing noise?"

"Well, that's easy," grinned Terry. "If bees *didn't* buzz, they wouldn't be bees, would they?"

185

Daffy Dog

Daffy Dog was a big, friendly dog with floppy ears and a loud bark. Everyone in the village knew Daffy Dog and liked to stroke his silky ears and pat his head.

Daffy was very fond of people, especially the postman who remembered to bring him a bone every Friday.

Daffy lived in a large kennel in the back garden. He was quite happy there, but he would have been happier if his kennel did not have holes in it! When the wind blew Daffy felt quite chilled; when it rained, poor Daffy got wet.

One morning Sidney Squirrel saw Daffy looking very damp and miserable, so he and two friends decided to repair Daffy's home. The three squirrels spent a whole morning mending the kennel, putting on a new roof and painting it.

Daffy was so pleased and excited he couldn't wait until the work was finished, and went inside for his lunch, his tail wagging merrily.

I hope the squirrels didn't splash Daffy's new bone with paint!

The Flower Bear

"That's very strange," said Herbie Hare to his dad. "Yesterday when we came here to the meadow there were no flowers, but today the hillside is covered with blossoms!"

"Have you ever heard of the Flower Bear?" asked Herbie's dad. "They say if you get up very early on a spring morning, just as the birds are waking and while the dew is still on the grass, you might see him with his magic basket."

Next morning Herbie got up before anyone else was awake and hurried to the sloping meadow which had been green and grassy the day before. Keeping out of sight and very still he waited... and soon saw the Flower Bear sprinkling flowers about him as he danced and sang!

Herbie ran home as fast as he could; now he could tell his father that the story was quite true!

The Bicycle

Clarence Clown had been given an old bicycle by the Circus Master.

"Perhaps you could use it in your act," suggested the Circus Master. "I'm sure it would make people laugh to see you falling off it!" he continued.

But Clarence Clown had an even better idea: on his day off he used the bicycle to ride into the country, where it was quiet and restful. There he made friends with the animals and plants that lived in the fields and woods.

It made such a change from the activity and excitement of the circus and Clarence felt very much better after his outings.

Can you see anything strange about Clarence's bicycle?

187

Bunny Indians

There was an old tree trunk in the Bunny family's garden. Sandy Squirrel had shaped it into a totem pole with his sharp teeth. At the top of the totem pole Sandy had carved a bird which looked just like his friend Horace Owl.

The Bunny children liked having a totem pole in their back garden. It suited them because they often played Cowboys and Indians. Mum and Dad Bunny had made the Bunny children a wigwam from long sticks and coloured cloth; Grandad Bunny had made them a tom-tom out of a barrel and some stretched drumskin, and they had collected coloured feathers to make themselves Indian headdresses.

When Uncle Fred Bunny came to stay with them the Bunny children wanted to play Cowboys and Indians all the time. Poor Uncle Fred soon realised it wasn't much fun being the only cowboy in the Indian camp!

188

Along the River-Bank

It was a warm summer day and Porgy Pig and Bill and Bob Bear were out walking by the river. Shadows from the trees danced on the water, which seemed to sing as it flowed between the flowery banks. On their way the friends passed Water Rat sitting outside his front door, dozing in the sun; they saw Dinah Duck floating happily downstream followed by five fluffy ducklings.

"Oh, I wish *I* lived on the river," sighed Bob Bear.

"Why? What would you do with yourself all day?" asked Porgy Pig.

"I would sit on the bank and eat honey-flavoured ice-cream," said Bob Bear, grinning at his two friends. "I would also bathe my paws in the clear, cool water..."

"Bob! Watch where you're walking!" cried Bill Bear.

But it was too late! Bob Bear had been so busy talking that he had walked straight off the river-bank and into the water. Luckily Bill Bear and Porgy Pig were able to pull Bob out of the river.

"On second thoughts," Bob told his friends later that day, when they had helped him dry his soggy clothes, "perhaps I'll stay here to eat my ice-cream after all!"

Bearland Park

Brownie Bear's job was to look after Bearland Park. He kept the park tidy and swept up the leaves when they fell from the trees in autumn. He patrolled the park every day to make sure it looked neat and clean.

Usually Brownie Bear was very gentle and friendly, but one thing always made him very cross. That was finding litter and rubbish in the park. So when, one spring morning, he saw Sid and Stan Squirrel dropping things in the grass, he went over to speak to them straight away.

"Please don't drop things on the grass," he boomed. "It makes Bearland Park look very untidy."

"But Mr Bear," said Sid Squirrel, "we didn't mean any harm. We were scattering seeds on the ground so that more flowers will grow here in the summer."

"Sowing seeds!" beamed Brownie Bear. "Well, that's all right then! I hope every one of your seeds will grow and blossom. Please come to Bearland Park as often as you can, to see how they are getting on."

Silly Kitten

Julie had lost her pet kitten. She searched the house from top to bottom. She looked in the bathroom, the bedroom, the lounge and the kitchen, but Julie could not find her kitten.

Julie went outside into the garden and called: "Kitty! Oh, where are you, Kitty?"

Julie couldn't see Kitty, so she kept very still and listened, hoping to hear her.

As Julie listened she heard the builder's men working next door and the cars speeding along the road at the front of her house. But there was no sight or sound of Kitty!

In the next garden, one of the builder's men was lowering a bucket at the end of a rope when he caught sight of something unusual. A kitten was peeping over the top of the bucket!

"How did you get in there?" gasped the man.

"Miaow!" answered the kitten.

"You must be Julie's Kitty," said the man. "I think I'll take you home before you get into any more mischief!"

The Pixies' House

Simon spent his school holidays staying at his Uncle Ben's farm. Simon liked to get up bright and early to hear the birds singing their dawn chorus. Sometimes he would catch a glimpse of rabbits playing at the bottom of the big field. Often, while Uncle Ben was milking the cows, Simon would feed the hens. Then it would be time for breakfast in the farmhouse.

One sunny morning, after they had eaten, Simon and Uncle Ben went for a long walk. They walked across the big field and into the pine wood beyond.

"Some pixies live in this wood," said Uncle Ben. "Would you like to see their house?"

"Yes, please!" said Simon.

Simon followed closely behind Uncle Ben until they reached a small clearing between the tall trees. There, Simon was amazed to see the tiny wooden house, and neat garden, where the pixies lived.

I wonder, were there any pixies at home?

Gathering Acorns

Selina Squirrel knew that she would have to collect a good store of acorns for the winter when snow covered the ground and she would not be able to find food easily. The trouble was that Selina's furry legs were very short – and the acorns were a long way up!

"I think I'm going to have to work hard," she said to her friend Bluebird, who was sitting on a branch above her.

Bluebird had an idea! "If I hop up and down like this, on the oak tree branches, perhaps the acorns will fall down," she said. "That would help you, wouldn't it?"

When autumn came they found her plan worked, and Selina soon had a big store of acorns.

A Welcome Visit

Aunt Betsy Bunny often visited the Botanical Gardens in Coneyland and always saw something new and beautiful there. The gardens were full of colour and Aunt Betsy saw plants there she had only seen in picture books.

There were cacti from distant deserts, orchids from oriental gardens and tiny flowers that only grew high up on snowy mountains.

One spring Aunt Betsy hurt her leg and the doctor advised her not to travel while it was getting better. The next week a yellow van arrived at Aunt Betsy's house: when she looked out of her window, there was the Head Gardener from Coneyland!

"We know you can't visit us for a while," he said kindly, "so I've brought you some plants to cheer you up and remind you of your visits to the Botanical Gardens."

What a lovely surprise for Aunt Betsy!

Ready for the Storm

On the plain the animals had been listening to the weather forecast. "There will be heavy rain," it said, "particularly in the plain, where it will go on for weeks."

King Lion called a special meeting. "We shall have to get ready," he said, "as I know most of you can't swim very well. The camels and elephants must gather wood to build a big boat – an ark – and the monkeys will collect vines from the jungle to bind it together. The birds can paint it cheerful colours, so everyone will be able to see it for miles and come to safety."

All the animals agreed and began collecting and building at once. In two days the enormous boat was finished and pairs of creatures hurried aboard, looking very worried.

When the ark was nearly full a pair of hippos galloped towards it, looking very happy. "We've just heard," they said, "that a strong wind has blown all the rain away. We're safe!"

How many different animals can you see in the picture?

Bouncing Rabbits

For two weeks during their summer holidays Barry and Bobby Rabbit helped Farmer Fox. Their job was to get up bright and early and go into the farmer's field and pick the mushrooms. Farmer Fox gave Barry and Bobby a sack each in which to collect the mushrooms.

On the first morning the two rabbits were carrying their sacks to work when Barry suddenly had a good idea. "Instead of us carrying the sacks, why not get the sacks to carry us?" he laughed. In no time at all the two rabbits had climbed into the sacks and were bouncing through the grass on their way to work!

When they reached the meadow the two little rabbits began collecting the white mushrooms. It was hard work – but it was fun too, seeing who could pick the faster.

By eleven o'clock Barry and Bobby were beginning to feel tired and very hungry. The sun was warm on their fur and the two sacks were half full. Then the two silly rabbits both jumped into their sacks again and bounced all the way back to the farm!

Farmer Fox was not very pleased to see the fresh mushrooms squashed and broken – and they all had mushroom soup for the rest of their holiday!

What the Moon Saw

One night the moon went walkabout in the sky. He peered into all the windows and was very pleased when he saw the little children fast asleep. He loved to see them safely tucked up in bed with their toys. Of course he did not manage to peep into all the windows he passed because some had heavy curtains drawn across them. The moon had been unlucky with quite a number of windows as he sailed along and he was getting quite cross, when all at once he came to a window with pretty, flowered curtains. He looked into the room and was delighted to see an old, white-haired man sleeping peacefully, with his hat still on his head!

"Well now," said the moon to himself, "here's a funny sight. I expect he has been to a fancy-dress party and forgot to take off his tall hat before he went to bed." The moon smiled gently, and before sailing on blew some special moon-dust magic into the room. "Now you'll have a wonderful dream which will stay with you all day long and make you feel young again!" the moon whispered, as he drifted away, happy again.

Big Ideas

Two elephants called Big Bing and Big Ben were bored. "What shall we do?" moaned Big Bing. "I'm getting tired of eating doughnuts all day long."

"Let's try a bit of skate boarding in the local park," suggested Big Ben.

"I've tried it," groaned Big Bing. "They've put a sign up. 'No Elephants on Skateboards allowed in this Park'."

"I've an idea!" said Big Ben. "Let's take a plane to India and see our cousins."

"But elephants are banned on aircraft," cried Big Bing.

"Yes. But we can go by *Jumbo* Jet!" said Big Ben.

Cuddly Bear Crescent

Percy Pig was a town postman. He liked his job because it took him out into the fresh air and gave him plenty of exercise. He also enjoyed meeting the different animals as he delivered their letters.

There was Willie Woodmouse who always hid in an old tree-stump at the top of Cuddly Bear Crescent and jumped out to surprise Percy! Lots of animals lived in Cuddly Bear Crescent: Boris Badger at number one, Patricia Panda and her mother at number three, and a large family of monkeys next door to them.

Opposite, at number two, lived Mr and Mrs Bear and their children; Percy Pig enjoyed delivering their post. That was because Barnie and Bertie Bear had a banana slide in the front garden! If he was not late, Percy would stop to watch the two small bears having fun and games on their banana slide.

Can This Really be the Moon?

The Professor visited the moon quite often in his super invention, the cigar-shaped spaceship which ran on spinach juice. Sometimes he took the young animals. Of course, the Professor was used to all the mountains and craters on the moon, but the visitors were always surprised.

"Can this really be the moon?" young Bert asked. "I thought it was made of green cheese."

"I assure you," said the Professor, "this is the moon..."

Just then, little Bunty vanished down one of the craters and, though it was all her own fault for being too curious, the Professor set out to rescue her. He knotted Bert's long scarf with his own and threw this lifeline over the crater edge. Bunty grasped it and was quickly hauled up.

"I don't like the moon," she said, looking shaken. "I want my Mummy. Please take me home."

Bert said she was a spoil-sport but the Professor was growing tired of the moon, so he packed them into his spaceship and they were all safely home in seconds.

199

Samantha's New Umbrella

Samantha the white rabbit was going to her friend's birthday party. She had brushed her whiskers and put on her pretty pink dress and was ready to go.

Then she looked out of her bedroom window and saw that it was raining outside. But Samantha didn't mind because she had a new umbrella made of leaves and she couldn't wait to try it out.

So Samantha put on her yellow waterproof boots and her yellow waterproof hat, picked up her leaf umbrella and walked out into the pouring rain. It kept her perfectly dry.

Poor old Tom the Tortoise was outside her front door, trying to shelter from the rain, but he only had his shell to keep him dry.

"Hum!" he mumbled. "I wish they made umbrellas for poor old tortoises like me."

Happy Jogger

One day Podgy Pig looked at himself in the mirror. "Goodness me!" he squealed, "I am getting fat!" He set his alarm for six o'clock so he could go for a jog before breakfast.

When he was about halfway round the park Podgy felt hungry. "It's lucky I've brought a little snack," he said, and found a quiet place to eat it.

Podgy hasn't actually lost any weight, though, because jogging makes him even more hungry for breakfast.

Grandma Bunny's Present

Grandma Bunny lived in Bobtail village. She had a very nice house with a garden full of lovely flowers.

Grandma Bunny had a grandson called Baby Bunny.

Grandma Bunny hadn't seen Baby Bunny for three days and she was wondering where he had got to. She went down the path and stood at the gate to see if she could see him.

Who was this coming along the track? My goodness! It was Baby Bunny, carrying a big carrot!

"Hello, Grandma," said Baby Bunny. "As I haven't seen you for so long I thought I'd bring you this little present."

"Why, bless you!" cried Grandma. "Seeing *you* is the best present I've had since I don't know when!"

Scarecrow in the Woods

Two naughty little bunnies thought they would play a trick on their teacher when she took the class for a nature walk in the woods.

"We'll hide behind one of the trees," Billy whispered to Hazel. "She won't miss us until she starts counting us before we go back..."

Little Hazel agreed. They let the others go ahead, and when the teacher was telling the class why it was important to let the wild flowers grow in the woods, they crept away!

What fun they had, these naughty runaways. Then what a fright they got when they suddenly came upon a huge scarecrow! Billy was certain it was a wicked witch come to carry them off. Little Hazel began to cry and wonder if she would ever see her mummy again.

"If you let us go this time, Madam Witch," said Billy, in a small, scared voice, "we won't ever run away from our teacher again and we'll go straight back to her now."

Of course, the scarecrow didn't speak, but it looked so stern and fierce that Billy took Hazel's hand and together they ran through the woods until they found their teacher, who was just setting out to look for them. Weren't they lucky that the teacher was too tired to be really cross!

Sailor Bears

Toby and William were very sad. The next day was their birthday and their father would not be at home. He was a sailor on a big ship thousands of miles away.

When the postman came the next morning he brought a huge parcel, with strange stamps on it. "This has come from the other side of the world," he said importantly. "It's a surprise for your birthday."

Inside the wrapping was a set of instructions and everything Toby and William needed to make their own boat! They spent all week gluing and building, cutting out the stripy sail and fitting the mast.

Early the following morning Mrs Bear and the twins set off for the seaside with their new home-made boat. The breeze was gentle and the waves quite safe. Toby and William had a wonderful day sailing up and down the shore – being sailors just like their father!

Crocodile Bridge

The three monkeys were standing on the banks of the river. The river was very deep. And the current was very strong.

"We'd better cross at the wooden bridge," said the first monkey.

"Yes. It will be much safer than trying to swim across," agreed the second monkey.

"I can't swim anyway," admitted the third monkey. When the three monkeys reached the bridge they found it had been swept away by the river.

Luckily for them, a friendly crocodile called Eustace was passing by and he offered to help.

"I'll lie across the river, and you can all walk across me as if I were a log," suggested Eustace.

The first monkey walked across Eustace safely. But the third monkey was so frightened that the second monkey had to give him a piggy-back across.

"Thank you very much," chorused the three monkeys when they reached the far bank.

"Have a nice day," said the crocodile.

Oswald Owl – Signalman

Oswald Owl was very upset. News had reached him that the local farmer was going to cut down the tree which had been his home for years!

"I won't know where to go," he said sadly to his friends. "I might as well give up. Whatever has got into Farmer Jones to think of doing such a thing!"

"They want to build a signal box," said his best friend Ollie. "The tree is in the way."

Oswald scarcely stirred from his home and all his friends worried about him. Then Ollie, who was by far the cleverest, had a brilliant idea. He went to the old railway station and he found there just what he was looking for – a signal lamp in first-class condition. It was no trouble at all to carry it back in his strong beak.

In no time at all, the lamp was cleaned up, restored to perfect working order and then hung on a strong branch just outside Oswald's front door.

"No need for a signal box now!" laughed Ollie. "And, what's more, both Farmer Jones and the railway board have put you on their payroll!"

Dream-House

There was once a builder who grew tired of building ordinary houses. All his working life he had built the kind of houses which people wanted. He built bungalows and town houses and cottages and semi-detached houses and mansions which sold for a great deal of money.

"Now," he said to his wife one day, "I'm going to surprise you. I'm going to build a fantastic house which won't sell because it will not look like an ordinary house. But I don't care."

This worried his wife, who was a very cautious lady and did not spend ten pence when five pence would do! She did her best to put her husband off the idea but he would not listen.

The next week he began building his dream-house. True to his word, when it was finished it didn't look like any house he had ever built before.

"You will never sell it," said his wife crossly. "That house will be the ruin of us!"

"I don't care," he said. And he planted banks of gorgeous sweet-smelling flowers on either side of the long flight of steps that led to the front door.

His wife was wrong about the strange house. People came from miles around to look at it until, at last, a millionaire offered such a huge sum of money for it that the builder agreed to sell!

Now he is busy building another dream-house which is even stranger and more fantastic than the first one!

Rock-a-Bye Baby

Betsy Bunny was not very pleased when her mother told her to take care of her new little sister. "I don't want to," she said crossly. "I want to play."

"I'll put Baby in her pram and you can watch over her whilst I bake a nice jam sponge for tea," said Mummy.

Betsy went out to play with her best friend. When Baby began to cry she didn't pay any attention. Baby went on crying and crying. At last Mummy rushed out. "Your little sister is crying," she said. "Why don't you rock the pram?"

Betsy shook her head, and Mummy picked up Baby. Baby stopped crying and suddenly Betsy wanted to hold her little sister.

"I'll have her," she said and she held out her arms.

"I thought you wanted to play," said Mummy, smiling.

"I did!" said Besty. "But now I think it would be fun to take care of my little sister. I'll sing her 'Rock-a-Bye Baby' until she falls asleep!"

Stew-Time

Pancho Pig had invited three friends to supper. He went to market very early and bought fresh onions, turnips, swedes and carrots. At home he put on his chef's hat and apron and began to prepare a vegetable stew. When suppertime came his kitchen was filled with lovely savoury smells!

Pancho and his three piggy friends ate every scrap of food and his guests said it was the best meal they had ever tasted.

"Good!" laughed Pancho, feeling very pleased. "Now perhaps you three would like to do the washing-up!"

Toot Takes a Holiday

Early one spring morning Toot made up his mind to take a holiday. It wasn't his real holiday, which was usually in winter when he was not needed so much.

"I'll get away before anybody is up," Toot told himself. "When they miss me it will be too late."

So, with a happy smile on his face, the little engine got up a good head of steam and chugged out of the yard. He knew exactly where he was going. There was an old branch line which wound round the hills into the country and Toot knew that was where he longed to be.

The birds sang to him as he chugged along and the lambs put their noses over the low wall and called out friendly greetings. "Hi, Toot! Have a lovely day!" one bleated.

"Enjoy yourself!" cried Ralph Rabbit.

"I will, I will," Toot called back. And he really did! When the sun grew hot he stopped and looked about him and took in deep breaths and felt quite wonderful! Of course, when he finally went back to the yard he was in all kinds of trouble, but Toot just went on smiling. He knew, you see, that no matter what they said, he had had a lovely holiday.

Clever Rex

Poor Mrs Rabbit was tired. She had such a long way to go to the shops each day – and when her shopping-bag was full it took a very long time to get home again.

Rex Rabbit liked to make things and had his own saw and hammer. He wondered how he could help his mother with her shopping.

"I know," he cried. "What we need is a cart!"

"Could you make one?" asked his mother.

"Certainly," replied Rex. "I know where there is enough wood – and a pair of wheels." Rex set to work and sawed and hammered all that day.

Next morning, when Mrs Rabbit picked up her shopping-bag, she found Rex at the door with his new cart! "In you get," he said proudly. "I'll pull you to the village – and you *and* your heavy bag back home again!"

Now Rex always uses his cart for trips to the shops, and also collects wood and vegetables in it. What a clever rabbit!

The Inventor

Professor Dogwatch loves inventing things – anything at all. When his friends come round they always ask what it is? Just recently Maurice Mouse did just that.

"What does it look like to you, Maurice?" said the Professor.

"It looks like a machine for taking potatoes, washing them and cutting them into chips."

"Well, that's exactly what it is," said Professor Dogwatch, relieved that someone had found another use for his wonderful-looking new machine. After having some tea Maurice Mouse went home to bed. But the professor immediately started drawing ideas for his next invention!

Sonny Bunny

Sonny Bunny was the untidiest rabbit in the world. His mother was always telling him to put away his toys. But Sonny much preferred to spend his time roller-skating outside his home.

One day Sonny's mother was not feeling well. "I'm afraid you'll have to tidy the house for me today," she said. Sonny decided it wouldn't take very long if he hurried.

But as he raced about he stepped on one of his roller-skates and landed flat on his back with a plant on top of him! "That will teach me to put my things away!" he groaned.

Silas Snake

Tommy Squirrel was scampering through the grass when he heard a strange whistling. A moment later he almost bumped into Silas Snake, who was looking rather unhappy.

"Is that you whistling?" asked Tommy in surprise.

"Yes," moaned Silas. "Every time I try to hiss, out comes this silly whistling instead. If I open my mouth very wide, could you please see what is wrong with my throat?"

"Very well," agreed Tommy.

When Tommy looked into Silas's mouth he couldn't see *anything* wrong. He thought for a moment.

"Perhaps you're just whistling because you're happy," suggested Tommy.

"Of course," said Silas, looking brighter. "I never thought of that!"

211

The Tea Party

One afternoon Mrs Rabbit baked a very special chocolate cake for the children and her husband.

The cake had eight – no – nine cherries on top and some rich, creamy icing inside. The children could not take their eyes off the cake and Susie counted the cherries four times. But Mrs Rabbit pretended that the cake was not for eating.

"Drink up your tea, children," she said, smiling. "And finish your plates of bread and butter."

"What about the cake?" Susie asked. But she ate up all her bread and butter before Mrs Rabbit could tell her to again.

At last the big moment came. Mrs Rabbit picked up the cake knife and slowly and solemnly cut four big slices which she put on the plates.

It was the best chocolate cake in the world, and all the better because everybody had had to sit patiently waiting for a taste of it!

212

Scamp's Circus Trick

Scamp the Dog lived in a brightly painted caravan with his friend the clown. They travelled with the circus to a new town every week and made lots of friends.

Scamp enjoyed travelling and meeting people, but he wanted to be a proper circus performer. The trouble was he had no tricks that people would pay to see. He tried juggling with three red balls, but he couldn't catch them. He tried walking along the high wire, but it was such a long way up he felt dizzy – and had to scramble down quickly. He even tried magic tricks, but none of the hats he used seemed to have white rabbits in them!

One day he was telling the circus master how he felt. "But you can do one thing better than anyone – the elephants, seals, horses or clowns," the man said kindly. "You, Scamp, can *jump!*"

Scamp now performs in the circus every evening. He wears a special ruff round his neck and jumps through a big hoop . . . and the children think he's the best circus performer of all.

Gustav

Gustav was a big old oak tree. His roots dug deep into the earth and his branches lifted up towards the sun. Gustav's trunk was huge and round and gnarled.

In the winter, Gustav's branches were bare, but in the summer he had many leaves, and birds built their nests in him and sang songs from his branches. Voles had their home amongst his roots. In the autumn, Gustav bore many acorns which the squirrels ate.

Gustav was a friend to all the animals and people too came to visit him.

Around the base of Gustav there was a circle of coloured stones. And in the summertime a circle of yellow flowers grew up around Gustav. No one knew who had planted the flowers. Except Gustav.

Surprise Ending

Thelma Rabbit was very surprised when she saw her husband hurrying up the garden path at two o'clock in the afternoon. She was even more suprised when her usually hard-working husband marched straight into the sitting-room, sank into the best armchair, and put his feet up.

"I'm home, Thelma," he cried, smiling broadly.

"So I can see," said his wife, not realising that she was still clutching the kettle she had meant to polish.

"I'm home for good," her husband went on. "Now, make me a nice cup of fresh carrot tea, and I'll have one of your crunch biscuits to go with it . . ."

"You will not," said his wife. "That is – you won't get anything until you have told me the worst! They must have sacked you – and after all these years of faithful service, too . . . Oh my goodness me!"

"It's the other way round, girl," chuckled her husband. "I've won the Bunnyland pools! Now, what about that nice cup of tea?"

"Right away, my dear," said Thelma, smiling in her turn. "And *two* of my crunch biscuits to go with it!"

Turning Over a New Leaf

One day the Professor told his wife that he was going to turn over a new leaf. "In other words," he said, "I am going to help more in the house. I am not going to spend so much time with my books and my inventions!"

His wife was very pleased to hear this because she was growing tired of seeing her husband's nose stuck in some book. "Now let me see," she said. "You could begin by helping me in the kitchen. This is my day for clearing out the cupboards."

"Delighted, my dear," said the Professor. "Leave them to me!"

Now, normally the Professor's wife would have stayed to see what her absent-minded husband was doing. But just then a neighbour came and invited her next door for a cup of tea. "I won't be long," she said cheerfully. "But you can make a start..."

The Professor really had no idea what to do with the things in the first cupboard. There were so many packets and bits and pieces. But after giving the matter some thought he decided to take the lot outside and

stack it up in the shed. That would clear out the cupboards as his wife had intended and get rid of everything quite quickly. So, huffing and puffing because he was not used to such hard work, he trotted to and fro from kitchen to shed, balancing packets and boxes, one of top of the other, as best as he could.

Imagine his wife's surprise when she came home. It is true that all the cupboards were bare but there was a trail of biscuits and cereals all the way from the kitchen to the shed. Instead of being furious with her silly husband she blamed herself for ever thinking he could turn over a proper new leaf.

Pip's Magic Moment

When Pip the Terrier ran onto a football field the crowd usually laughed and the referee chased him off the pitch. But one day he was picked to play for the Terrier All Stars. It was a dream come true.

As soon as Pip got the ball he ran fast towards the goal, pushing the ball with his nose. When the goalkeeper came out to stop him, Pip ran between the goalkeeper's legs and scored a great goal. The crowd cheered loudly.

When the game was over, Pip fell asleep in the dressing-room and dreamed his magic moment all over again.

The Echo

Colin Cat was playing his guitar. "Tra-la-la," he sang, "tra-la-lo." Suddenly he heard an echo. "Tra-la-la," it went, "tra-la-lo."

Colin played a few more notes. "Tra-la-la, tra-la-lo," he sang. Back came the echo: "Tra-la-la, tra-la-lo."

"I like it," purred Colin. "If only I could take that echo around with me." A moment later a little canary fluttered down onto Colin's guitar and sang, "Tra-la-la, tra-la-lo."

"So you're the echo!" grinned Colin. "Come on, let's sing a duet."

217

Eli and Barney

There were bright posters all over town telling the animals that the funfair was coming to Bearland. Eli, the baby elephant, asked his friend Barney Bear if they could go together.

The sun was shining when the two friends arrived at the fairground. There was lots of noisy music, coloured balloons and ice-cream. When Eli asked if they had any honey-flavoured candyfloss for baby elephants a kind bear made him one specially.

Barney took Eli for a ride on the roundabout and they laughed at their funny shapes in the hall of mirrors. They bought each other a little present: Eli bought Barney a red lollipop and Barney bought Eli a funny hat.

Their last ride was on the big dipper. When their car began to rush downhill at top speed Barney nearly lost his lollipop – and Eli had to hold on to his new hat with his trunk!

Baker Bunny

It was a breezy day in spring and two young squirrels were playing their favourite game. Steven Squirrel would run as fast as he could and his friend Simon would try to catch him.

Rudy Rabbit had been playing the game too, but he couldn't understand how the squirrels could play for so long without feeling hungry! Rudy was waiting for Baker Bunny, who always came through the wood at tea-time. The big basket he carried round his neck was filled with delicious cakes he had made that morning.

When Baker Bunny appeared Steven and Simon ran up to him with their money in their paws; they knew that for two squirrel pennies they could buy three iced buns – one for Rudy Rabbit and one each for themselves. After they had eaten, Rudy Rabbit felt much better. He even had enough energy to collect the crumbs together and feed them to the wild birds.

Jake the Snake

Mike Mole was busy shopping one day when he saw Colin Cat outside the supermarket. "Hello, Colin!" said Mike. "I haven't seen you for ages. Where have you been?"

"I'm very busy rehearsing for the pantomime at the Animal Theatre," explained Colin. "Would you like to come with me and have a look round?"

It was quite dark inside and the stage looked very big and empty. There were curtains on both sides and lots of lights and wires. Suddenly they heard a hissing sound close behind them. Mike Mole jumped in surprise.

"Don't be afraid," said Colin Cat, grinning. "It's only Jake the Snake, who plays the part of the monster in our play!"

"I'm sure he does that very well indeed," said Mike politely!

Bimbo the Dog

Bimbo the Dog didn't like living in one place all the time. He didn't have a proper kennel and, when it rained, he sometimes got very wet!

One day he found a battered old dustbin. It wasn't very beautiful, but it was clean and dry – so he decided to move in.

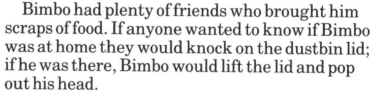

Bimbo had plenty of friends who brought him scraps of food. If anyone wanted to know if Bimbo was at home they would knock on the dustbin lid; if he was there, Bimbo would lift the lid and pop out his head.

Cuddles the Cat was Bimbo's most welcome visitor. Cuddles lived with a poodle who never ate any of the bones her master gave her . . . so Bimbo soon had a large store in his dustbin, thanks to Cuddles.

Farewell Party

Harriet Hippo had received an invitation to live in a big zoo in a far-away town. She was very proud and excited.

Harriet decided to hold a party for all her friends the day before she started her long journey. She made invitations and painted them with jungle flowers, asking all the animals to a special tea.

They had a wonderful afternoon, but Harriet grew sad when it was time to say goodbye. "I would like something to remind me of you all," she said.

"I have the very thing," cried Tufty Bird. "I'll take a colour photograph with my camera – then you will have a reminder of all your jungle friends when you are far away."

Harriet was very pleased – and the photo is now by her bed in the big zoo. She looks at it often and thinks of her friends.

Joe and Bluebell

Joe was a rabbit who loved to go walking in the countryside. He walked to the fields every day to collect some juicy grass to eat. Sometimes Joe found a carrot or two.

There was a donkey called Bluebell in one of the fields, and if Joe had a spare carrot he would take it along for Bluebell to eat. Bluebell and Joe would talk for hours. They would tell each other exciting stories of their youth. Two or three friendly songbirds would perch on the fence to listen to their tales.

When Joe and Bluebell had finished talking, the birds would sing a thank-you song and their bird music would make Joe and Bluebell feel very happy and contented.

The Magic Candlestick

Bertie Bear had been reading all about Aladdin and the magic lamp. All Aladdin had to do was polish his magic lamp and a genie would appear to carry out his commands.

"I wish I had a magic lamp, too," said Bertie Bear.

Later that day when Bertie was playing in the garden he found an old brass candlestick in the shrubbery. "I'll borrow some of Mum's brass polish," he said, "and polish and polish the candlestick. You never know. It might be a *magic* candlestick!"

As Bertie polished the candlestick he was thinking to himself, "If a genie appears I'll ask for some honey cakes for tea."

At that moment his mum came back from shopping and seeing Bertie polishing the candlestick said to herself, "My little Bertie's a good bear. I'll give him some of his favourite honey cakes for tea!"

223

Hubert's Treat

Hubert Hippo was very lazy. He was so lazy that he really couldn't be bothered to wash very often, or clean his teeth, or polish his nails. Being dirty was a bad habit that Hubert was too lazy to do anything about.

When it was Hubert's birthday he sat in his muddy pool as usual and waited for someone to remember. His friends hadn't forgotten, but they didn't bring him any presents! They had all decided it was time Hubert was cleaner, so they had saved their pocket-money and paid the monkeys to give him a beauty treatment!

Hubert wasn't very happy with the idea, but, being lazy, he stood in the clear water while the monkeys scrubbed his thick skin with scented soap and rinsed the mud from between his toes. His eyelashes were combed and his teeth brushed until they sparkled. Hubert looked wonderful!

Since that birthday treat Hubert has found he is much happier being clean – and he has just as much fun!

Merry Musicians

You may think the woodland animals spend all their time making nests and burrows and collecting food, but you would be wrong. Walter Weasel had learnt to play the accordion. The rabbit twins, Ken and Ben, played the trumpet and banjo and Maurice Mole had a pair of soft drumsticks that could beat out a rhythm on almost anything.

Whenever there was a party in the wood the four friends put on their special clothes and got together to make music for the other animals to dance to.

Good Medicine

Whenever Philip Mouse went to stay with his Aunt Emily he always enjoyed himself. There were lots of exciting places to explore and corners where he could play hide-and-seek with his cousins.

One day Philip began coughing, so his Aunt Emily bought him some cough medicine.

"Take one spoonful of the cough mixture just before you go to bed," said his Aunt Emily, "but don't forget to shake the bottle first."

But Philip was so busy planning his next adventure he wasn't really listening to his aunt's instructions!

Just before bedtime Aunt Emily found Philip swinging to and fro on the pendulum of the grandfather clock.

"I forgot to shake the bottle," squeaked Philip Mouse, "so this is my clever way of shaking up the medicine!"

225

The Greedy Crow

Crosville Crow was always hungry. He ate the seeds from the farmer's field and the swill from the piglets' breakfast trough. When the kittens weren't looking he even drank the cream the milkman had left them for a special treat. One day he went too far. He ate the pea from the whistle on the Meadow Express!

Without a pea the whistle wouldn't work, so the animals didn't know when the train was coming. They were late for school, or missed the shops. Everyone was very cross with Crosville!

The train driver decided to put a new steam whistle on his engine. When it was ready he asked all the animals Crosville had upset to come for a free ride.

The driver pulled a cord and the new whistle hooted loud and long. Off they went, chugging through the countryside, with the steam whistle singing a happy tune.

226

The Flower Fairy

Sarah loved wild flowers. On her walks through the woods with her dog, Perky, Sarah tried to count how many different kinds of flowers grew there.

One fine summer day Sarah and Perky had taken a picnic with them on their walk. The sun was shining and the birds were singing. The dark green grass was like a soft carpet with a bright pattern of colourful flowers woven into it. Perky was scampering about, sniffing and wagging his tail. Suddenly he stopped running and started to bark.

"What is it, Perky?" asked Sarah.

The little dog was sitting on a small bank, looking very pleased with himself! All around were the loveliest flowers Sarah had ever seen, most of which were quite different from the ones she knew. As Sarah came nearer she saw what Perky had found . . . a tiny wooden door in the side of the bank!

"I wonder who lives here," Sarah whispered. "Perhaps it's the flower fairy!"

When Perky and Sarah had finished their picnic they left an iced biscuit by the little door – to thank the flower fairy for all the beautiful flowers.

Talking Flowers

Pufftail Rabbit was hopping past a little stream which sparkled in the sunlight. "What a wonderful place to be!" he said.

"Yes, it is!" a voice replied. Pufftail jumped. He couldn't see anybody. "I'm Pufftail," he said. "Who are you?"

"My name's Hoppy," replied the voice.

"That water-lily is speaking to me! It must be magic," thought Pufftail. As he looked closer at the flower its petals sprang open and he saw a tiny green frog! "*You* must be Hoppy," said the surprised rabbit.

"That's right," the little frog croaked, "and you woke me up!"

Come and Get It!

Every morning Mrs Bunny cooked a pan of delicious porridge. When it was ready, she would stand at the kitchen door, pan in hand, waving her big ladle. Then she would shout, "Come and get it!" and her husband and children would come pelting down the stairs without even stopping to wash. When they had eaten every scrap of the lovely porridge they would often yawn and go back to bed without as much as a thank you!

Mrs Bunny grew very upset and worried by their bad behaviour, and decided to do something about it.

"Next time they come pelting downstairs for their porridge," she thought, "it will have plenty of pepper and mustard in it!"

So, the very next morning her family got a nasty shock. And they quickly learnt to be less greedy and to say thank you!

New Homes

The rabbits had lived in Willow Warren as long as they could remember. Ron and his little sister Rachel had been born there.

One autumn a terrible thing happened. So much rain had fallen in the wood above that water began trickling down into the warren! Soon Mrs Rabbit's clean floors were pools of mud and the chairs and table in the kitchen started bobbing about like ducks!

Their friend Mr Mole, who lived underground next door, was having the same problem. "My bed floated out of the front door last night . . . while I was asleep in it!" he squealed. "We really will have to find somewhere else to live."

Mr Mole and Mr Rabbit spent several days looking for new homes. At last they found the perfect place. There was a big house for the rabbit family and a smaller one for Mr Mole and, best of all, they were on a little hill where the rain wouldn't come in.

The Rubbish Bird

Dusty, the rubbish bird, was the most miserable bird in the forest. "If only I wasn't so ugly," he would say to himself as he perched on the branch of his favourite tree after a morning's work. "If only they didn't always think of me as a nasty, smelly, rubbish bird…"

One morning a bright little bird perched on Dusty's branch. "My," he exclaimed, "you do look miserable!"

"I am," said Dusty. "Nobody wants to be friends with me. They only speak to me when they want their rubbish cleared."

"I'm speaking to you," said the little bird. "And I haven't any rubbish for you to clear. So cheer up!"

"The truth is," said Dusty, "that I'm tired of being a rubbish bird. I want to be something different – but I'm so ugly…"

"Why not be something different?" said his new friend. "I have an idea. Why not be a guard-bird? You look big and fierce enough to scare away anything. And just to get you off to a good start – come home with me and guard my nest of little ones. The missus would love a break."

Dusty thought it was a wonderful idea. Now he is very much in demand and ever so popular with the little ones he watches over – especially when he pulls funny ugly faces and makes them laugh!

The Train is Late

"That stupid train is late," grumbled Midge Mouse. "That means we will all be late for our rehearsal."

"We should have gone by bus," said Rory Rabbit. "I told you so!"

"The train is not late," said Miss Piggy, in a stuck-up voice. "I wish you would all stop grumbling. I'm going for my usual singing lesson with Professor Thrush and the train always gets me there in time..."

At this the members of the orchestra fell silent. But not for long, and in the end Miss Piggy grew very annoyed. She tossed her head and said loudly, "If you don't keep quiet I shall tell the engine-driver to leave you behind..."

Before the friends had time to think of something clever to say, the little train came chug-chugging around the bend. Miss Piggy looked at her splendid new watch. "Right on time!" she exclaimed.

"I hope she doesn't get into our carriage," Rory whispered as they started to climb aboard.

How could he know that Miss Piggy always had a ride beside the engine-driver who kept a soft pink velvet cushion for her to sit on!

Nice and Dry

One day Max Tortoise was out walking with his friend Tiny Rabbit when it began to rain. Max Tortoise's shell kept him dry, but poor Tiny Rabbit got very wet indeed.

"I'm afraid there is only room for me under my shell," said Max, who felt sorry for his little friend, "otherwise you could shelter under it and keep dry like me."

Indeed, Max was so upset at seeing Tiny Rabbit get wet that the next time they went out together Max remembered to take his big umbrella. "Now if it rains you won't have to worry," he said kindly to the little rabbit.

On their way home dark clouds covered the sun and a strong wind began to blow. Big raindrops splashed down and Tiny Rabbit shivered.

His friend smiled, opened the big umbrella and held it up... but Max was so tall the umbrella was too high up – and poor Tiny Rabbit was *very* wet again when he got home!

Piggles the Pig

Piggles was different from the other pigs on the farm because she had two mud-coloured marks on her side, just above her tummy. No matter how hard she scrubbed, Piggles could not get rid of those marks.

One very hot day all the young pigs had been playing in the muddy puddle at the edge of the field. When they went home Mrs Pig was very cross to see them all splashed and dirty. All except Piggles, of course, because she *always* looked muddy!

Sometimes, looking different is a good thing!

232

Buddy Bunny's Packing

Buddy Bunny was going on holiday with his cousins.

"Have you thought what to take with you?" his mother asked, three days before the holiday.

"Of course!" said Buddy. But he hadn't.

On the night before his holiday his mother got out his case. "I'll put in your towel and new sponge bag and soap," she said. "You give me all the things you are taking."

Suddenly Buddy was in a panic. He went over to his cupboard and pulled out scarves, woolly mittens, odd socks and other bits and pieces.

"Goodness!" exclaimed his mother. "I thought you were going to the seaside. You will be hot in your winter clothes!"

Poor Buddy! How he wished he had sorted out his holiday things earlier. But his mother soon came to his rescue. "Never mind," she said. "All your summer clothes are in the top drawer. You bring them to me, and we'll soon get the packing done. Then you can go to bed early so as to be nice and fresh for the start of your holiday."

The Toy Train

Rupert the Rabbit had a toy train. There was a red engine and three yellow trucks which Rupert pulled along with a piece of string.

Every day Rupert the Rabbit had lots of adventures with his toy train. When bedtime came, Rupert used his bed as a tunnel several times before resting his train in the corner of his bedroom.

One day Rupert's dad made a train shed for the train, out of a cardboard box. So before Rupert went to bed, he could put his toy train to bed first.

Baby Bear

Baby Bear was lost in the Big Wood. He'd been walking for nearly an hour and he didn't know where he was.

Mother Bear had said: "Don't go far. And be sure you're back for tea."

"Oh, I do wish I'd listened to Mother Bear," moaned Baby Bear. "I would be home now and eating some of her lovely honey cake instead of being lost in the Big Wood."

He was just about to lie down and go to sleep when a bumble-bee came buzzing by.

"Excuse me, Mr Bumble-bee," said Baby Bear, "but can you guide me home, please?"

"Of course, Baby Bear," buzzed the bumble-bee. "It's easy. Just follow me. I can smell Mother Bear's delicious honey cake from here!"

Grandma Bunny's Shopping

Grandma Bunny had such a bad cold that the doctor had told her to stay indoors.

"Yes, doctor," said Grandma Bunny. "But if I stay indoors, who will fetch my shopping for me?"

"Ask any friendly rabbit who is passing by," said the doctor. "I'm sure they won't mind fetching your shopping for you."

So Grandma Bunny waited by her front door. But every time a rabbit hurried by, Grandma Bunny sneezed. And the rabbit was gone before she could even say, "Excuse me!"

Luckily for Grandma Bunny, a friendly tortoise called Timmy plodded slowly by. Timmy said he'd be happy to fetch Grandma Bunny's groceries for her.

It took him a long time, as tortoises can't walk very fast. But Grandma Bunny was delighted. "Bless you!" she said. Then she sneezed.

"Bless *you*!" said Timmy.

235

The Castle

The two squirrel brothers, Sam and Scamp, were climbing oak trees in Badgers Wood, looking for acorns. One of the trees was very tall and when Scamp reached the top branches he could see an old castle in the distance.

"Sam," he cried, "I can see a castle. Shall we go and explore it together?"

"What a good idea!" squeaked Sam.

The two squirrels scampered through the wood until they could see the castle. It looked very much bigger now they were close to it! The door was open, so the brothers crept inside. There were suits of armour, swords, shields – and lots of cobwebs! There was also a bag of assorted nuts on the floor.

"I wonder who these nuts belong to?" Scamp said in surprise, and he picked up the bag.

"They belong to *me!*" said a muffled voice, very gruffly.

"Good gracious!" gasped Sam. "There's a squirrel living in that suit of armour!"

These stories also appear in:

Bedtime Tales
Goodnight Stories
Slumberland Tales
Sleepytime Tales
Night-time Tales
My Bedtime Stories
Bear's Bedtime Book
Funny-Bunny Bedtime Stories